DARKEST FEAR

by

KIMBERLEY RAINES

CHIMERA

Darkest Fantasies first published in 2000 by
Chimera Publishing Ltd
PO Box 152
Waterlooville
Hants
PO8 9FS

Printed and bound in Great Britain by
Caledonian International Book Manufacturing Ltd
Glasgow

All Characters in this publication are fictitious. Any resemblance to real persons, living or dead, is purely coincidental

Copyright © Kimberley Raines

The right of Kimberley Raines to be identified as author of this book has been asserted in accordance with section 77 and 78 of the Copyrights Designs and Patents Act 1988

DARKEST FANTASIES

Kimberley Raines

This novel is fiction – in real life practice safe sex

Ladies
Are you lacking in self-confidence?
Are you fed-up with being a doormat for your partner?
Come and learn the art of
DOMINANCE
with an expert

Chapter One

Alicia felt a jolt of desire hit her middle as she took Kevin's overcoat from him at the door; a single glance told her he was already blatantly aroused. It was hard to believe, but she had really done it; the sexiest man in the office was really here in her flat. His cold grey eyes bored through her, and she shivered with a belated sense of apprehension, but thrust it aside. He was married, and had a reputation as being a bit of a philanderer, but as far as she was concerned that was both the challenge and the safety net. Taking a deep breath she closed the door on the outside world.

His hands bit into her shoulders as he leaned down and kissed her. He didn't close his eyes, neither did she, and lust billowed tangibly between them. There was nothing refined in the way his hands gripped her shoulders, held her there while his tongue played along her teeth, then thrust deep into her mouth, pushing her tongue aside. She felt a moment's claustrophobic panic, and tensed. He retracted his head slightly, malicious amusement sparkling within the flecks of silver in his strange eyes. When he spoke his breath warmed her open lips. 'Scared?'

'Of what?' she said breathlessly, hearing a slight taunt in the tone, and feeling desire blossom even more strongly at the hint of threat. She leaned forward to kiss him again, but was left discomfited as he turned casually away as if he had not noticed.

'Go over there, by the window,' he said abruptly.

She went, confused, but obedient.

'Now, undress. Very, very slowly. I want to watch.'

Alicia felt that strange jolt again. He was deliberately belittling her, yet it was not anger that blossomed, but something else. Something deeper, more primitive. As she undid the buttons of her silk blouse, one by one, he wandered to the dresser and poured himself a glass of red wine, never once taking his eyes from hers. Trapped in his avid gaze Alicia licked her lips, something telling her this was not a good time to insist that he repeat the action for her. She wished she had knocked back a glass before he had arrived, but she had not, intending to share the wine with him during the softening process that usually preceded sex. But it was too late now, and she belatedly realised that with Kevin Mellinton she was a foregone conclusion, ergo, did not need softening.

Without the comforting haze of alcohol she felt strangely exposed to her own confused feelings, and felt uncomfortably aware that this was going to be an experience somewhat different to normal. But then, Kevin had hinted as much during their clandestine challenges at work. She wanted to walk over and turn on the CD player, put on something sultry and moody, but she didn't. This was to be done in silence, stone cold sober.

She wasn't looking at him now, but felt his eyes on her as she slid the blouse down over her shoulders very, very slowly, shuddering as the light pressure of the silk slid against the hair follicles on her arms. Almost every hair on her body seemed to be tingling with a charge like static electricity as the blouse fluttered to the floor in a rich green puddle. Now goosebumps chilled her torso. She breathed in deeply, watching his reaction as she stood, knowing what she looked like with her full cleavage straining against the tiny, lacy bra.

She reached behind her for the zip of her skirt, which opened with a soft sigh. She bent to slip the skirt slowly down to her feet, then stepped carefully over the waistband, trying not to catch the high heel in the fabric. She reached for the buckle to her shoe.

'No. Leave those on.'

Kevin's voice was abrupt, his very arrogance sending the juices flowing. Oh, God, he was wonderful. She had known he would be. She was captivated by the hawk-like gaze that never left her body. His erection was thrusting proudly against his trousers, but he didn't move, didn't touch himself.

She shivered again as she undressed herself, feeling strangely violated, as though his hands were all over her body, touching, smoothing her pale skin. The waistband of the suspenders dug into her skin, an alien sensation, but when Kevin had presented her with the beribboned package in a sly moment when she was alone, she had felt exhilarated, because no one had ever bought her anything like that before. Of course she had to wear them, show him that she appreciated the gift; besides, it was obviously expected.

'Slip the knickers off,' he said, and now she could hear a faint tremor in the husky depth of his voice. She had never been asked to do this before. There had always been a kiss and a grope on the settee, hands ripping frantically at clothes. This leisurely, solitary disrobing was faintly disturbing.

She slid the elastic of the silk French knickers down over the clasps that held up the stockings, and stepped out of them. She stood in bra and stockings and high heels, and was shocked at the blast of excitement that hit her middle. She must look like a tart; she felt like one. She had never experienced anything like it before.

'Now turn away. Face the window. Lift your arms up high. Spread your legs.' His commands were like her actions, slow and deliberate, and there was nothing seductive about them. He was using her for his own pleasure, and she was obeying because she wanted to. At any moment she could just say 'no', but she knew that would be the end of it. Erection or no, she sensed he would simply take his coat and walk out of the door. She wasn't sure why she cared, cold bastard that he was.

She opened her legs, wobbling slightly on the high heels, and felt the dampness between her legs chill slightly. Again she had a mental impression of what she looked like, standing there with her white cheeks like two globes either side of her deep crack.

'Twist your hips,' he said. 'One way, then the other. Slowly.'

She did so, as far as she could, perched on the high heels, lifting one cheek, then the other, in a gyrating motion. She heard glass tinkle and knew he was pouring himself some more wine. She felt slightly cheated. 'I'd like—'

'Shut up.'

His tone bit her into instant silence. She was faintly

shocked at her response. He was talking to her as if she was a dog, yet something stopped her from complaining. She was not under duress here, she could put her skirt back on any time she wanted, and to her surprise, she didn't want. What she couldn't understand was why. What was it in his arrogance that made her want to carry on pleasing him? Yet her body knew no such hesitation. It was fired with need in a way she had never experienced before.

'Now rub your hands down your body. Press your tits together, then down your sides, up the cheeks of your arse, nice and slow. Round and round, that's good. Very good.'

She felt chuffed at his slow, deliberate praise.

'Now put your hands on your hips and bend down. Right down, that's it. Lift your head back, stick your bottom out. I want to see it. All of it. Every sweet, juicy inch.'

She stood there for a moment, and heard faint movement behind her.

'Hold the window sill.'

She did as she was told and was shocked to feel warmth at the mouth of her sex just a second before he thrust inside her, hard as a rock, more brutal than any man had ever been with her. She gasped with shock, with an explosion of sexual excitement, feeling the roughness of his clothes against her, knowing he was within seconds of coming.

There was no finesse about the way Kevin rammed into her, about the way his hands grasped her thighs for better purchase. Her displays had made him as ready as he ever would be; he didn't need hands touching him to get him hot. He needed mastery, that was all. He thrust hard, in and out, nearly lifting her from her feet at every movement, and she felt it building inside him, ready to burst.

Because her legs were spread wide, Alicia had no control over any muscles. The rough penetration was painful, but clutching hard at the white-painted sill she found her lack of control as erotic an experience as she could recall, the pain itself an aphrodisiac.

Finally he gave a great shudder and shot his seed inside her, and as she felt the warmth of his balls pulsing against her clitoris, she gave a faint gasp of something akin to relief as she felt the strength of his orgasm.

'Jesus!' she sighed as he finally slid out, depleted.

Kevin slapped her bottom. 'Nice arse,' he said. 'Now go and rustle up some grub, there's a good girl.'

She stood up, wincing, and turned, hands on hips, suddenly irritated. 'You are a conceited arsehole, Kevin!'

His lip curled. In exasperation she reached for her clothes, but he stopped her. 'Like that. I like to watch.' Torn between the desire to hit him or thank him for the compliment, she stormed into the kitchen in high heels, stockings and bra, and began to rustle up some grub as ordered.

Alicia felt like stamping around the kitchen, but it was hard to stamp in ridiculously high heels and little else. After a while she began to smile to herself, and the ache between her legs was almost a badge of honour. What a stud! Christ, she'd never felt so goddamned horny. She had known from the first instant she saw him in the foyer that she was going to have him, but she hadn't expected to get him this easily. What the hell kind of wife did he have? One who wasn't interested in sex, in which case this was understandable, or was Kevin just so sexy she was unable to keep up with his demands? She shrugged. It didn't really matter. He'd been turned on merely at the sight of her, and the feeling was mutual. She didn't have to like the bastard. She was smirking with self-satisfaction as she took his food into the living room on a tray, almost as if they were a married couple, for God sake. She put the tray on the small table and turned around.

'Where are you going?'

'To get mine.'

'Come here. Take off your bra and stockings.'

She undid the catch and let her large breasts fall free, then sat beside him on the sofa and unbuckled her shoes, sighing with relief. He held a hand out for the stockings, and she handed them over, puzzled.

'Turn around. Give me your hands.'

'I don't think—'

'Do it, or I'll leave right now.'

She turned, crossed her hands behind her back, and he wrapped one stocking around her wrists several times. Something went zing between her legs as he worked. She had never been tied before. She felt him pull the knot tight. 'What are you doing?'

It was such a silly question, he didn't deign to answer. He yanked the free ends of the stocking around her middle, pulling her wrists tightly into the small of her back. 'Breath in hard. Harder. That's better.'

She inhaled so hard her breasts jutted proudly, and her middle sank in smaller than she had ever seen it. He pulled the knot tight around her waist, ensuring that she stayed in that hourglass condition.

'Now you won't be hungry,' he said with a grunt of

satisfaction.

She could only breathe in constricted gasps. 'I don't think—'

'Shut up. Open your mouth.'

He stood up and picked up her silk panties from where they lay, abandoned on the floor, and he was looking into her eyes as he stuffed them, bit at a time with one finger, into her mouth. She sat there and let him do it. Then he took her other abandoned stocking, wrapped it around her mouth and tied it off. She gagged faintly on the silk knickers, then stared at him, stunned. She had known what he was going to do before he did it, but complied because he had asked. She wondered where it came from; this need to please him. After all, she hardly knew him. She knew he was a high-flying salesman for the Corporate Division, and everyone spoke about him with a kind of awe, but that was all.

He turned on the television, picked up the tray and ate the dinner she had prepared, watching the football, his eyes gleaming with excitement when someone scored. If she hadn't been watching so closely she would hardly have seen the excitement. Christ, he was a cold fish. Alicia sat beside him, trussed into a sex toy, hungry, desperate for a drink and gasping for breath. She was thoroughly bemused. It was as if she didn't exist. Yet for some reason she didn't dare move or make any kind of complaint. She was not afraid he would be angry, she was afraid he would simply up and leave if she didn't please him; and for some reason, the thing she most wanted to do in the whole world was please him.

Yet when the match finished he switched off the

television and turned his attention to her with an abruptness that told her his mind had been preparing itself for a while. It was the strangest thing she had ever seen. One moment he was watching the match, next moment his prick was stiff between his legs, bulging against the zip of his trousers like some obscene animal trying to get out of its confines.

He stood up.

Never taking his eyes from her, he began to strip. His tie, his shirt. She saw his chest was not hairy, but hard and masculine, as were his arms and legs. Then he removed his shoes, his socks, and slid his trousers and pants down over a neat bum and muscular thighs. Now his blue eyes were sparkling.

'Ready, darling?' he said.

She nodded. Oh yes, she was ready. Just watching him did that.

He pulled her onto her knees on the floor and turned her to face the seat. Then, spreading her legs, he began to massage her thrusting breasts, and all the other places she had often imagined the feel of his hands – including one she had not thought of. She jolted and made faint shocked noises as a finger slid into her anus.

'You're dry. I didn't think of that. I expect you've got some cream in the bedroom. Stay there. Don't move.'

He stood up and walked away. Alicia leaned against the sofa, feeling the tightness of rope around her middle and the rough fabric against her breasts, and panic in her heart. God, he was going to bugger her, that was what he was going to do. Half of her mind was repelled; it wasn't something she had ever anticipated doing, yet she stayed there, waiting, her legs apart as he had left them, until he returned carrying a tube of hand cream.

He knelt, shuffled between her legs, keeping them apart with his thighs, and his finger slid inside her with a cold, soft touch. She winced, but it wasn't with pain. Just the shock of entry. As his finger slid in and out, preparing her, she began to writhe under his touch, never having experienced anything so erotic before. Every time his finger entered her she shuddered, every time it exited she gasped through the gag.

Desire burned her into a quivering mass of compliance. He was going to bugger her, oh yes. Then she felt the heat of him press up against her. She knew a moment's panic, but realised if she cried out he would stop. She was torn between the fear of what was going to happen and the strangely erotic sensation it engendered in her. Besides, she was curious. Other people did it, so she waited for what seemed like an eternity, feeling the pressure increase, and suddenly there was the strangest sensation she had ever known as he pressed in. Her arse widened accommodatingly, lubricated with her own hand cream, and the feel of him pushing further and further in that most private of places was a crazy mixture of pain and pleasure, and most deliciously decadent. Her bound hands writhed behind her back. Oh, God.

Kevin slid in and out of her a few times, and the tight ring of her virgin arse felt like heaven. He moved in and out gently until he felt the muscle relax, become accommodating, then began to push harder, feeling the tightness of her up and down the full length of his penis. Yeah, this one was okay. He had known she would be. Desperate to please, he could always tell. They sort of made cows eyes, the ones he knew he would get in the end.

He pulled her back towards him slightly as he pleasured himself, the blood really pumping his prick into an iron bar, raising his balls deliciously. He reached around her tiny middle and up to those ripe breasts, and with his hands full he slid back and forth, sinking into the tight elasticity which contracted beautifully at every stroke. Better than a wank. Far, far better.

She was making noises now, and her body was shuddering. He slipped a hand between her legs and his fingers slipped in the dampness there. He pulled her back against him.

Then, once again he felt the buzz, and forgot to pleasure her as he brought himself to his peak, hanging on to it as long as he could. He pulsed inside her, the tight ring of her arse making the ejaculation almost painful. They hung there for a moment, joined. Then as he shrank her body squeezed him out with a soft plop.

Kevin lifted her to her feet and walked her through to the bedroom, a persuading hand gently slapping her bottom. 'You're so nice and accommodating, sugarplum, I'll think I'll stay the night. How about that? I guess we ought to get to bed fairly pronto, though, as I have to be at the management meeting first thing in the morning.'

When Kevin walked into the boardroom he fairly waltzed with the euphoria from that long night's loving, in spite of his tiredness. He tried not to think of the following days, when Alicia would be looking out for him, waiting on stairs or in doorways for that quick fondle she was now used to. They always felt possessive for some reason, after a bonking session. He felt vague feelings of regret. She had been so very easy to manipulate. Accompanied by a faint stirring in his groin he recalled clambering onto the bed, how he had pulled her head between his legs and asked her to suckle him into fullness once more. It was so very comforting, and required little effort on his part. She hadn't been too keen when her soft lips roused him to another erection and he ordered her to circle him with her tongue, but all he had to do was threaten to leave and she sucked harder, and fought against her inclination to gag when he thrust her head down for his ejaculation.

Now she would be expecting more of the same, and for a while he would be happy to comply, although it was never as good as the first time. After a while someone new would enter his orbit, and his magnetism would find a new target. It always took them a while to realise there was nothing permanent in these games. Didn't the women talk amongst themselves? He gave a private grin. Of course they didn't. Unlike men, women didn't boast of the conquests, but almost seemed embarrassed by them. He couldn't understand that.

By the evening, of course, he would be tired, but it was a good kind of weariness and he looked forward to the comfort of his own home. As he thought of his wife his gaze softened. Esther would rub his feet, run him a hot bath so he could soak, and if he felt pleasantly tired, he might even find the energy to make love to her. She deserved that much from him.

Frank Brachlyn, the chairman, couldn't help noticing the almost instantaneous level of tension that arrived in the boardroom with Kevin. The men because they saw him as a threat; they really couldn't understand what it was he had that they didn't, and the women because they were angered by desires which had no place in a modern woman's agenda.

Frank knew all this, while remaining absolutely baffled to the exact nature of Kevin's sexual magnetism. It was nothing he could categorise. The man was fairly good-looking in a classic kind of way, clean cut and presentable, verging on six foot, and looking stylish in whatever he wore, but none of that was out of the ordinary. No, it was something deeper; something more basic and primitive, something very predatorial that could assess a woman's sexual experience and availability in an instant, even while he was discussing interest rates and market trends with her. Yet he still couldn't understand why the women fell for him. One look at those cold eyes should have put them off for life.

Thus, for various reasons every person in the room loathed the sight of him, but the reason he still remained employed by High Corp plc lay in the fact that the very magnetism they loved to hate was often put conveniently to use on the company's behalf. As he sat down, late as always, there was a sudden shuffling of paper and clearing of throats.

'Kevin, my boy,' the chairman said with a flash of white teeth. 'We've just been talking about you. It seems that the FairBank deal is having teething troubles. They're getting cold feet. I was just letting everyone know that I have decided to take their directors out for a meal. You know the ropes: wine, dine, and soften, and bye the bye, when I've had a bit to drink, let them know that we've received another offer which we're considering in the light of their present lukewarm state.'

'Have we?' Kevin asked with interest.

'Of course not. I don't want to lose this one, but it wouldn't do them any harm to believe we're back on the market. If we play hard to get it will inject new enthusiasm into their bid. Put them on their toes, make them think they're fighting for it, Kevin, my boy. What do you say? I really want your support.'

Kevin's eyes gleamed at the challenge, but that was the only sign of enthusiasm he gave away. But inside he was euphoric. They needed him, the bastards. 'Sounds reasonable. Why not? When are we going to do it?'

'Saturday. It's all organised. I trust you don't have any prior engagements?'

'No, nothing of any importance.' Kevin leaned back, stretched his arms behind his head and crossed his legs comfortably, his thoughts taking a new turn. He had been intending to push Michelle, that new secretary, into the final confrontation, and see if he couldn't wangle the weekend with her. Would she or wouldn't she? He snapped his brain into gear. That would have to wait on the back burner; this was his livelihood, his big career move.

Frank slapped Kevin's knee with a jocular comradeship he did not feel. 'That's great, my boy. And I thought this was the very opportunity to let the wives out of the cupboards, eh? Show the FairBank crowd that we are a happy bunch with traditional family values. Quite important, these days.'

Kevin blanched fractionally. 'Oh, I'm not sure that

Esther can—'

'Don't you worry your head about it,' Frank said. 'I've had my secretary invite the wives personally, and your little Esther has agreed to put off her proposed family visit until after the weekend. Just take her out shopping, dear boy, and buy her a new frock for the occasion. And tell her not to worry, we won't eat her. You ought to get her out a bit more – get her polished up a bit.'

Kevin's heart sank into his boots, hearing a warning in the tone. Wives were an essential part of these functions; but he swallowed his discomfort admirably. 'I'm sure she'll enjoy it,' he said, his fixed smile attaining a slightly strained appearance. Damn the man, he knew Esther was no socialiser. She would dry up and go all mousy and cling to him as she always did, cramping his style. Hell.

But it was *fait accompli*, and they all knew it. The men smirked down at their papers, enjoying his discomfort, but the women grinned openly. After all, had they not all seen Kevin's poor little dab of a wife? You could almost understand why he felt the need to bonk everything in sight. God knows how he came to get saddled with her. Perhaps she'd had money, or perhaps he felt sorry for her, but whatever the reason, she was going to be out of her depth at this party, and with any luck she would sink like a stone and drag Casanova bloody Kevin with her.

The board meeting carried on above Kevin's head. He could think of nothing but the excruciating realisation that if Esther came she was going to let him down. She was great at home, but a real liability when it came to socialising. How could he get out of it? Perhaps he should persuade her to be ill? He grimaced; she couldn't dissemble at all. She was hopeless at lying. He would have known instantly if she'd ever had an affair or something, because she was just too damned naïve to hide it from him. That was one of the strengths of their marriage. It made a man feel safe knowing that his wife was there for him, that she wasn't running around behind his back. But a social function? He had been dreading this moment, waiting for it, and now it was finally here. What was he going to do? She was nothing like these executive broads with their predatory smiles. Nor was she like the wrinkled leather bags the directors were married to. Between them they would eat her alive, and enjoy it, the bitches.

But there was also the fact that he really didn't want anyone to talk to her about what he got up to on those executive weekends, and long evenings when he worked late and stopped over in the city. Of course, she probably knew what he was up to; she might not be socially geared, but she wasn't stupid. He had a reputation for being a lady's man when she married him, and she must have known that wouldn't change overnight. That was another of her strengths, that she accepted a man's needs without continually harping on about it. But there were rules, and one was that the wife was not regaled with details. He was going to have to stick to her like a glove to keep her out of the reach of the bitches, and behave himself all night to boot, which was a pain. But the damage was done, he thought grimly, and he would just have to live with it.

On the day of the dinner Esther was as excited as a child. She knew these business meetings often involved social events, but so far she had never been invited to one, although it had always been on the cards. Now Kevin was finally rising within the firm she was very happy for him, and even if she felt a bit insignificant beside those highly confident career women, she would do her utmost not to let him down. She had bought a new dress, assisted by Kevin, as she hadn't known what kind of thing to buy. And if she looked a bit on the dowdy side, she supposed that he was trying to make her dress the same as the other wives who were mostly older than her, and that was a very kind touch. Anyway, these dull browns were fashionable right now, the lady in the shop had assured her.

Upon their arrival at the venue her excitement was dampened by the sight of the ranks of expensive cars outside the hotel, and the ostentatious glitter of jewellery within it. She realised instantly that Kevin hadn't realised it was to be such a formal event, or he would surely have persuaded her to buy something with a little more panache.

'Esther, *darling*. So nice of you to join us.'

Esther smiled nervously at the chairman's plump wife, Amanda, whose vast family jointly owned the majority of the company's shares. Then she endured a two-cheeked embrace before being left standing as Amanda, duty performed, swept past and homed in on one of her cronies.

Kevin took a firm grip on Esther's arm and led her in. Her heart sank as she gradually realised there were three kinds of women present: the wives of businessmen who exuded all the confidence of ranking officers, the younger female executives who had nothing feminine about them whatsoever, and herself. She felt as dowdy and uninteresting as they believed she was, but inside she felt a quiver of resentment. Just once in her life she would like to show them all, and Kevin. Only she didn't know what she would like to show them. But something. If only she knew how.

She would have been surprised to know that she was not as disliked as she supposed. Most of those who knew Kevin realised that though his wife was not what they would have expected of the most lecherous man in the company, perhaps it was just as well, as no one else would have put up with him. And they did admit she seemed to be very nice, classy almost, in a quiet sort of way, and perhaps she deserved better in a husband.

Esther, though, not realising she engendered such sympathy in those present, felt her confidence shrink to the size of a peanut during the course of the evening.

For Kevin, from a business point of view, the evening was undoubtedly a success, in spite of his having to stick to Esther like a limpet. He managed to sweet-talk the manager of FairBank into another business meeting, one he made sure was an overnighter in the city, and came away happily content to be mothered by Esther for the remainder of the weekend, which had already been ruined as far as assignations were concerned. He needed that now and again, just as relief from his high-flying life. In bed he responded as well as he could to her sexual overtures, but was nearly asleep when he slid away from her in the dark.

Esther stayed awake a long time thinking about the evening in its awful entirety, but in particular about meeting one woman by the name of Chrissie. In spite of the smile, which had all the charm of a cobra about to strike, Esther knew the woman was vindictive for some reason and yet she had given Esther just what she needed. In her handbag – her own personal space where Kevin would never venture, through some misguided sense of ethics – lay an embossed card.

She hugged this information to herself. Lessons in self-awareness and assertiveness were just what she needed, but she had finally realised what she wanted to do. She would like to surprise Kevin at the next business function, show him the kind of wife she really could be given the opportunity.

Back in work, Kevin had another surprise. Personnel had taken on a new secretarial assistant by the name of Gloria. She was tall, rounded in all the right places, and had the most amazing shock of curly red hair he had ever seen. He desperately wanted to know whether she had another shock of curly red hair down below. His imagination pictured it in detail, but he really had a hankering to see for himself. The only problem was Gloria herself, who for some reason seemed to be standoffish. No matter how charming he made himself she responded politely, giving him no indication whatsoever that his charm was having its usual effect. He was sure that beneath the cold front she was as warm and wriggly a lay as he had ever enjoyed, and was probably playing hard to get. And if she was intelligent, which he thought she probably was, she would undoubtedly hold out for some kind of inducement, i.e. a raise. His teeth bared in an avaricious smile. If she was playing games, he was a past master at changing the rules. But then, he had plenty of time, and Michelle had recently, against his expectations, been making all the right signs. Each in its turn, he thought smugly.

Chapter Two

Even though she could have quoted the message verbatim, Esther stared at the card, feeling butterflies fluttering in her stomach. It had seemed such a logical move in the comfort of her own home, but here and now was a different matter. She turned it over. On the other side the embossed card detailed the name, Madam Tisset, a telephone number and the address, outside of which she was standing.

Ladies
Are you lacking in self-confidence?
Are you fed-up with being a doormat for your partner?
Come and learn the art of
DOMINANCE
with an expert

She had consulted Jenny, a long-standing friend, about the card, including her misgivings about the manner in which it had been acquired, and also whether Kevin would really appreciate what she was doing. Jenny had pooh-poohed her misgivings, said even if Kevin didn't want it, it was about time she stood up to the male chauvinist dickhead she had married (she knew Esther well enough to be honest), and said even if he didn't approve, after the event it would be too late. And anyway, Esther needed to regain some of the self-confidence she used to have before

Kevin relegated her to housewife. It was about bloody time. Then she had phoned up Madam Tisset and made the appointment for her.

Esther realised dismally that Jenny was right. For some reason her few years of marriage to Kevin had not been all she'd expected. It had been very obvious, after the short but determined courtship, that the marriage was dull for him, too, otherwise why would he be running around with other women? She sighed. She couldn't even do this properly. Jenny had done the hard bit; the phoning. All she had to do was arrive, and even that she found difficult. She was sure she didn't use to be so spineless.

She knew she was at the right place because there was a small bell, above which a sign proclaimed this to be the residence of Madam Tisset. Was that as in French or English, she wondered, and took a step back to look up. The building that surrounded the grim barrack-room door looked like a warehouse. It was constructed of blackened bricks, and had a vaguely sad, unused air about it. This was definitely not a good idea. She took another step back, suddenly filled with a burning desire to turn tail and run.

'Stop.'

She froze without realising she had indeed turned to go. The word had not been shouted, but was a command all the same. She turned slowly. The woman behind her was not so much big, as powerful. Featureless in the dusk, and disguised by a dark plastic raincoat tied tightly around her middle against the chill wind, she radiated authority. 'Oh, boy. You really are under the thumb, aren't you, dear?' Esther sensed amusement in the rich, husky drawl. 'You only have two choices, you know; to carry on being the good little wife for the rest of your life, or to take control of your life now. Only you can decide.'

It was November, and the freezing cold was sapping whatever small amount of courage had been summed up to get her this far. Esther thought longingly of her warm safe living room with the co-ordinating decor and the easy-clean carpet Kevin had chosen. He wouldn't be there, though, he was at some conference or other, as he so often was these days. She felt instantly guilty for being pleased at the thought, but she had learned a while back that the word conference could cover a whole multitude of sins.

The woman walked forward, opened the door and flicked a switch. Harsh yellow light spilled out from a bare bulb. Esther noticed that the woman was older than she sounded, had bright red lips, and wore exceedingly high heels. She had been expecting some young, bouncy, health freak with a black belt in something nasty.

'You made it this far, dearie. Go the rest of the way. You won't get a second chance.' Then the casual attitude dissipated. 'You have to choose... now.' Madam Tisset walked inside. She paused, waited with her head cocked to one side, then shrugged, and the door began to close.

Esther stepped forward as though she had been shoved in the back. 'Wait! Please wait. I – I need to do this.'

Madam Tisset stood back wordlessly to let her pass, and Esther could feel the uncomfortable pounding of her heart as the door closed behind her with a reverberating thud. It had a sort of finality about it. What had she let herself in for? She had now entered the forbidden zone – there was no turning back...

The woman patted her shoulder in a motherly fashion

and set off down the corridor. 'It's all right, dearie, don't you worry about anything. We'll take it all nice and easy. Now, you come on in and tell me about this man of yours.'

'What has that to do with anything?'

'Everything. Tell me if I'm wrong. You were fairly self-sufficient. Had a job. Enjoyed life. Went out – drinks, parties, the like. Then this good-looking hunk of a man came along, swept you off your feet, gave you a romantic wedding, and suddenly there you were, his wife, the honeymoon period over. He liked his sex three times a week, a roast on Sunday and his slippers by the fire. Before you knew it you became his ideal wife. You don't have to go to work, you don't go out unless he takes you, and the biggest indignity of all is that you have to ask him for money.'

Esther was taken aback.

'You're not the first, dearie.'

'You make it sound awful. I should consider myself lucky that I don't have to work. He doesn't realise what he's doing, you see.' The words sounded slightly sanctimonious even to her ears, but Madam Tisset agreed without even sounding sarcastic.

'No, of course he doesn't. He's a man, poor dear. He probably thinks he knows what's best for his little wife, and talking won't make him change his mind. He's probably got a few good points we can eventually work on. But darling, if he's a model husband he's unique.'

As they were talking Esther followed her down the corridor, up some steps, and to another door, which opened to reveal a plush, if not over-decorated living room.

'W-where are the others?' she asked uncertainly.

'I don't do classes. I work with individuals.'

She was horrified. 'But won't that cost a lot?'

'Don't worry about it. I get paid for succeeding. You let me know if I fail.' Madam Tisset threw off her raincoat. She was wearing a sexy, red, body-hugging dress, and her bust spilled from the low top. She unlaced her ankle boots and collapsed on the worn settee with a sigh. 'God, those shoes kill me.'

Esther smiled nervously. 'Why do you wear them, then?'

'Image, dearie. That's one of the first lessons I'm going to teach you. Men see in a woman what that woman let's them see. It's all about image. Trust me! What I don't know about men doesn't exist. You see, this isn't only about training you, it's about training him and, believe me, ducky, he'll enjoy the experience.

'Right,' she went on casually, 'take your clothes off.'

'Pardon?'

'Strip.' She crossed her legs and rubbed her foot. 'Tell me if I'm wrong, but I'd guess you never used to wear such middle-aged frumpy rags before you got married. You decided it was time to mature, to do the married lady act, and hubby encouraged it.'

'Well, Kevin's very conscious of the image we present. He's right to be, you know.'

'Of course he is. Even men are right sometimes, but with you it was probably downright jealousy. He was afraid of other men taking a shine to you.' Her nose wrinkled. 'And if you go out looking like that you can be sure no other man will. It strikes me he achieved his aim, only the trouble is before you know it he won't look twice, either. Very soon he'll just see a dinner-maker, vacuum cleaner and baby-making machine when he looks at you, and he'll find his bit of pussy outside the marriage chamber. Ah, I see by your face he already does. Now, don't get me wrong, you can do the motherly bit for him if you want to, but you can also play several other parts, according to the situation at hand. Bring him back into the fold, so to speak. Let him know you won't stand for any nonsense. It can be fun, believe me.'

Esther gingerly removed her camel coat, slipped off her flat shoes, but balked slightly at unzipping the sensible wool dress in front of this strange woman.

Madam Tisset flashed her a look. 'All of it. You have to trust me or we'll get nowhere fast.'

Esther stalled. 'You're making it all so -- so sordid and sexual. I thought a self-confidence class would have something to do with being assertive.'

'You mean judo type crap? Dearie, leave the macho stuff to men. They can flex their egos for all they're worth. We've got other weapons, and they are sexual, make no mistake. Self-confidence is what you have inside you, it affects how you do things, how you look, how you feel. But it's also what other people imagine when they look at you. You can control all of that. Take you, here and now. The image I see is that of a housewife. It's boring. Let's get rid of it, shall we?'

Eventually Esther stood there in her naked glory.

'That,' Madam Tisset said with conviction, her pale eyes widening, 'is one nice body.' She stood up, took two steps, yanked a couple of cords, and suddenly the room seemed to be filled with wall-to-wall mirrors. Esther flushed bright red and instinctively tried to hide herself, an impossibility in the circumstances, as the gyrations of the naked woman in the multiple mirrors proved.

'Cup of tea?' Madam Tisset asked casually, switching on a kettle. 'Don't be afraid of yourself, dear. Lift your head up. You have a lovely body. Flaunt it, and even when it begins to sag a bit, like mine,' she grinned infectiously, 'still bloody flaunt it. What the hell… Sugar?'

'Um, one please.'

'Do you make love in the dark?'

'I… we… yes.' Her voice was quiet with embarrassment.

'Well don't.' Madam Tisset handed her a steaming, flowery mug. 'If you could see the stupid, fatuous expression on his face when he comes, you'd have less respect for his authority. You'd also have a bit more pleasure in the act, knowing you were the one who put it there. Have you ever come?'

'Of course I have!' She was indignant.

Madam Tisset gave a lopsided smile.

'At least, I think I have,' Esther added meekly.

'Then you haven't. Still, first things first. Walk around a bit. Move your hips, so. Stick out your chest. That's it. Great. Get natural. Get used to it.' Her eyes flickered with a hint of nostalgia. 'I used to look like that once. Oh well. Still nothing wrong with being a female when you get old. It's what makes the world go round.'

Esther sipped at the tea, and gradually the feeling of disquiet began to fade. She began to look at the body displayed in the mirrors with more interest. She was only a few years over twenty, her skin still creamy and firm, her breasts full without the hint of sag, her bottom well padded but not fat. Her naturally blonde hair hung in curls to her shoulders, echoed by the delicate golden curls between her legs, and her eyes seemed very green in the bright, artificial light.

She was undeniably beautiful.

Suddenly the room began to sway a little. With alarm she demanded: 'What was in the tea? You put something in the tea!'

'Just to help you relax, dear. Go on, look at yourself. Study every delicious detail. Bend over – look between your legs. That's what he sees.'

With surprising calm Esther did as she was told, realising that she had never actually looked at herself intimately before. She was surprised how large the lips of her sex looked from that angle, how small and tight and puckered her arse was, and how long her legs. The posture was an open invitation, and blatantly sexual. Intrigued, she opened her legs wider. Her breasts nestled happily between her thighs, and with her hands reaching to the floor, all her muscles were tight, accentuating every curve and line of her body.

Was that how Kevin saw her?

Madam Tisset leaned back in the sofa, put her feet up and crossed her ankles. 'Ever do that for your man?' she asked.

The upside down mouth in the mirror curved into a smile. 'He would hate me to be so – so coarse!'

'Because you're his wife and not his whore?'

Esther stood and swivelled angrily. 'Yes!'

'Men need a whore, too. If you're not it, then someone else will be.'

'Kevin doesn't want that kind of...' her voice petered out. She really didn't know what Kevin did want any more, and he certainly sought favours outside the marital bed. She hadn't needed Chrissie to tell her that. All Chrissie had done was let her know that everyone else knew what was going on, and that hurt.

'Stays late at the office, does he? Have there been rumours? Because there will be, and you can bet your bottom dollar they won't all be fiction.'

'That's why I'm here,' she admitted in a small voice. 'I want to tell him that he can't have me and other women. I can't let him do that.'

'That's the best way I know to lose him.'

'Oh... but—'

'You see, dear,' the woman continued, 'words are no use at all when you're talking about sex. You have to grow with him, you have to become what he wants, then he won't want the other women.'

'But I don't know what he wants,' she wailed. 'I was trying to be what he wants, and it isn't working!'

'You were trying to be one part of what he wants, because you didn't realise that men like everything in neat little compartments. The wife, the whore; the work, the home. I bet he's one guy in the office, another when he's out socialising, and something totally different with you. So you see, you have to do the same thing. A man is a very strange creature. He wants to be boss, but can't cope with responsibility. He acts like he's dominating, but what he really wants, deep inside, is to be dominated to take away some of his stress. What you have to learn is to let him be boss but make the decisions yourself.'

'It all sounds very complicated,' Esther said dolefully.

'It's easy. From what I can gather, your Kevin is a fine, strutting cockerel, crowing and boasting and ruling the roost. I've met many like that. For some reason they think that little bit of flesh between their legs makes them your boss and your better, and no amount of words will make him think any different. What you have to do is knock him off his perch and then allow him to climb back up in easy stages, so that once he gets there again he'll realise just what a very unstable perch it is. Let him do all the hard work to keep you.'

'And how do I do that?'

Madam Tisset smiled encouragingly at the positive question, even though it was spoken in tones of hesitation. 'The first thing you have to do is get him into a position of utter subservience, then you'll find what he's really made of. Now, before that happens, you've got to get some kind of self-respect going here. Let's sort out some clothes for you.' She walked over to another red curtain and drew it back to reveal a door. 'Come with me.'

The room inside was simply a vast wardrobe, but not like any wardrobe Esther had ever seen. She gasped. On one wall there were whips, gags, and leather things she couldn't think of a use for, and there were racks of garments made of leather, rubber, and studs. On the other side was a rack of flimsy stuff with lace. It was like a vast dressing-up box where she identified, amongst other things, outfits resembling those of a maid, schoolgirl, nurse...

She spun round, her eyes wide with shock. 'Good God,' she said. 'You're a...'

Madam Tisset was not noticeably upset or offended. 'The word is whore, dear. The oldest profession known to man. Or woman. It's quite an art form – if you're worth more than a quick blow-job, of course – because when they first come to you men really don't know what they want. The poor dears are confused, torn between their primeval needs and the conventions of society. Deep, deep inside their heads is a trigger for turning them to one or the other. You have to discover this trigger because often they have no idea what it is themselves. If your husband is knocking off other women it's because you haven't found his trigger, and he's searching other places for it. You have to find it before one of them does.'

'And how,' Esther said scathingly, 'am I supposed to do that?'

'That, my dear, is what I'm going to teach you.'

A couple of weeks later Esther realised just how much she was changing when Kevin breezed through the door, whistling. She could just smell cheap perfume on him, and recognised it for what it was. 'You have to keep up to date with things that matter to other people, dear,' Madam Tisset had said. 'You have to know your perfumes, follow the fashions, learn the right words. You don't have to be a fashion bimbo, of course, there's too many of those around already. You just have to know what's out there. It's an education. It's keeping abreast of things so when people are being catty you can cut them down with a couple of words. It's very effective.'

Oh yes, she knew that perfume. And if she went into the office, ten to one she would find out exactly who was wearing it. A small part of her didn't want to know, and the other wanted to go in and flatten whoever it was. She was in the kitchen with her apron on, which would not have worried her a few weeks ago, but now she felt the need to take it off. 'Had a good day, dear?' she asked, smiling.

Kevin didn't seem to notice her new dress. He gave her a perfunctory kiss and sighed dramatically. 'Hectic,' he said, reaching for the sympathy she could dispense so well. 'Make me a nice cup of coffee would you, Essie, honey?'

'I went to the class today, Kevin.'

'Class?' he said, with little interest.

'That one about self-confidence I told you about. The one with the French lady.'

'Good, good.' It was nice that she was taking the trouble to go to those classes. He was glad Esther was doing something other than moping around. She did seem a bit peaky lately. Perhaps it was time she had a baby; something to keep her occupied while he was at work. He ought to try again, tonight, only somehow he didn't think he could find the energy. Flopping wearily into his chair he kept the calculated expression from his face as he recalled his latest bout with Alicia. He had been right. Somehow the novelty had worn off, even though she'd been so anxious to please; she'd done everything he'd demanded, and then some. 'So what did she teach you today, honey?'

Esther smiled grimly. He would learn in good time. 'Psychology, mostly,' she told him as he picked up the paper and turned to page three. 'And sexual massage.'

'That's nice dear.' He reached absently for the mug she'd placed beside him. 'What's for dinner?'

'Your favourite. Roast beef with Yorkshire pudding.'

'But it's not Sunday. What will we have on Sunday if we have that tonight?' His complacency turned to confusion for a brief moment as the regimented order of his home life suddenly failed him. 'Did I hear you say something about sex?'

'No, I don't think you heard anything I said,' she muttered to herself. But she knew a moment of triumph at her small victory. Now it was her turn to whistle happily as she went back to the kitchen.

Chapter Three

As far as Melissa was concerned, Kevin discovered one evening that he was not required to make any effort at all. Still thinking of her as a prospective conquest, he found himself more than a little shocked when she took the initiative. He was working late at the office when she sidled in and locked the door behind her, giving him a glance of pure and unadulterated lust as she did so. He flashed a startled glance, recognised her intent, and instantly got the biggest hard-on he'd had in a long while. Just as well the desk was between them.

'What do you think you're doing?' he snapped coldly, appearing suitably unimpressed. It wasn't right that a woman should take the initiative.

She gave him a charming smile. 'I'm going to fuck you.'

'Indeed?'

'Indeed.'

His gaze should have chilled her, but she echoed his word, spicing it with a faint hint of amusement, and he saw for the first time the glint of steel behind the green eyes and pussycat face. He had just enough time to wonder fleetingly if this was one broad he should steer clear of, when she strode across the room. Even as he was pushing back the chair and rising to object she gave him a hefty shove which slammed him back into the seat. It was a director's chair on a five-caster base, and he sailed back towards the wall, startled, clutching the sides. She was stronger than she looked, and had also taken him off guard, but to his surprise a thrill of excitement quivered through his body at her aggressive action. No woman had ever pushed him about before. Always the dominant partner of any sexual encounter, the thought of being dominated himself was a scenario he'd never envisaged, and the novelty itself was an aphrodisiac. With interest he waited to see what she would do.

Like a cat stalking its prey she kept those green eyes on him while she stepped forward, one foot directly before the other, causing her hips to roll enticingly, and leaned down. Her tongue briefly lapped his tightly sealed lips, her eyes staring into his the whole time. As she backed away slightly he licked his lips, warmed by her tongue, and the brazen way her eyes were caressing him right down to his groin left him in no doubt at all as to her intention. Something nice uncurled inside him and he began to smile craftily. What did he have to lose? Sometimes, after all, it was better to go with the flow.

Melissa's slow smile suggested triumph, sending a small signal of warning to Kevin's brain. But he ignored it because she pushed his legs apart, knelt between them, and began to caress small circles on his shirt with a single, red-painted nail.

'You want me, I know you do,' she purred seductively. 'You've been watching me.'

His skin quivered beneath her touch, the finger slipping through the opening of his shirt and slipping into the hollow of his belly button. He jolted at the touch, gasping at the flood of sexual awareness generated by that simple movement. Again he saw that lurking hint of triumph, and had the unnerving suspicion that she was mocking him.

With a grimace of lust he reached out and grabbed her hair, intending to lift her up to him, but her hand instantly turned into a vice around a good handful of tight flesh at his middle. He almost shouted as her nails seemed to dig right into his abdomen, and he freed her hair instantly.

'Don't touch me, Kevin,' she warned. 'You wait to be asked. Understand?'

'Jesus! What the fuck—?'

'Good question,' she cut him off. 'The fuck is what I want it to be. How I want it to be, and when I want it to be. If you don't want that you say so right now and I'll unlock the door and walk right back out of here.'

He was frozen in place, knowing he could knock her right across the room if he wanted, but something stopped him. This was it. There wouldn't be another chance, he sensed that, and his ego would not deny him the opportunity that had just arisen. But a warning sounded in his mind. Was she a conquest or a bloody dominant cow? He wasn't quite sure, but a little devil whispered encouragingly, 'Go with the flow, Kevin, and when the time comes show her who's boss.' It was that simple.

They were staring at each other like two dogs about to scrap, then Melissa smiled. It was the smile that had attracted him in the first place; she really was very lovely, with a shiny crop of short chestnut hair, bow lips and neat white teeth. He had noticed that while she didn't have very much in the breast department, she did seem to be very fit and supple, which engendered further interesting speculation in his fertile imagination. To stroke his ego and take his mind off the way her nails were digging into him, he imagined her at his mercy, tied in an elaborate and intricate web of knots which left her various body parts available to him. The mental image appealed.

Sensing a fractional easing of his tension, Melissa relaxed her grip. 'Good boy,' she said. 'Now, stand up and take off your shirt. I want to see the goods before I buy.'

Kevin was taken aback. 'But we're in my office, I can't—'

'Afraid?' she taunted. 'Most of them have gone home.'

'The cleaners?'

'What cleaners, I've never noticed any around,' she said scathingly. 'Now, stand up and take off your shirt. I don't intent to tell you again.'

There was a snap to her voice which had him out of the chair like a shot. To his bewilderment, Kevin found himself removing his shirt as he had been told. There was a sort of risqué element about doing it in the office, and even while he was undoing his tie and slipping the buttons, his prick, which had wilted during the confrontation, hardened again dramatically. He decided that he hadn't jumped to the sound of her voice, but that he had decided to go along for the ride; see how bold she really was when push came to shove. Melissa perched on the edge of his desk, her legs invitingly wide. He could see the briefest hint of lace and his breath quickened.

'Now the rest.'

'Oh no, you can't be serious…'

But she gave him a look that made his hands slip down

to the waistband of his trousers. Even while he was fumbling with the zip, slipping the fabric down, freeing his erection from the confines of his pouch, she was watching him avidly. As he bent down to remove his shoes and socks he sensed her eyes on him almost like a physical touch, making his hair follicles rise and quiver with the thrill of anticipation, or nervousness, or embarrassment in case someone should come in. He wasn't quite sure what it was.

'You want me to show you what I can do so you can give me a star,' she accused. 'Now, legs spread, arms up.'

Her voice was lower, huskier than it had been previously, and he knew from the tenseness of her own body that she found him alluring. His ego rose a notch towards its normal level. He was attractive and he knew it; a fine specimen, hard in all the right places, without the least hint of middle-age spread. But standing in his office with his legs wide and his arms above his head, he felt a slight chill and shivered. God help him if any of the directors were still around. Even with the door locked he felt vulnerable.

Melissa stood up and inspected him closely, her fingers sliding down his flat abdomen almost to the bush of pubic hair. His cock twitched in anticipation, but she didn't touch. Instead she moved on around his body. His eyes followed.

'Keep your head still,' she commanded.

His face flicked forward and he stared ahead, sensing her behind him with far more excitement now that he could not see what she was doing. He felt the hint of her breath on his back, the lightest touch of her hand upon his tight buttock, and felt his erection jolt with anticipation. Touch me, he was thinking. Touch me, there... But she didn't. She carried her inspection full circle until once again she was leaning her neat bottom on the desk, staring at him speculatively.

'What?' he asked, somewhat irritably, maintaining his ridiculous posture for some reason he could not fathom. If the cow was being a fucking prick-tease, he'd show her a thing or two. After all, he was one hell of a lot stronger than she was, in spite of her attitude.

'I'm just thinking what I'd like to do with you, considering the possibilities, wondering how far you'll go,' she replied softly, calling his bluff.

'How far I'll go?' He gave her his lip-curling, snake-charming assessment. 'I think it's probably the other way around.'

Her eyes met Kevin's, and held them. As she brought out from behind her back a roll of brown packaging tape she knocked the complacency instantly from his face. For a moment he was almost panicked. One part of him thought he ought to handle the suggestion with the contempt it deserved; laugh, turn away arrogantly, deny he would be party to anything like that. But another part of him, for some stupid reason, shuddered with delicious anticipation at the sight. Why not? the little devil goaded. After all, he was stronger than her and could stop the game at any moment, couldn't he? And he was so very, very aroused. He hadn't felt so excited in years.

'Turn around and give me your wrists, if you dare,' she said softly.

His better judgement said 'no way, lady', but he was too arrogant to give way after her challenge, and with a certain amount of bravado did as she asked. He held his wrists crossed behind him as he turned, and presented them to her, slightly pushed away from his body. He felt the first pull of the tape stick to the hairs on his arms, then the bite as she wound it around again and again, pulling it tight, sometimes changing direction and winding it vertically between his crossed hands and arms until his wrists were encased in a thick wadge of tape. He pulled experimentally, and once again a thrill of excitement shivered up through his body as he discovered the tape to be absolutely immovable. His wrists might have been set in concrete.

She turned him around to face her and reached a cool hand to cradle his balls, which instantly tightened even further in anticipation. 'Now this is mine,' she purred. 'You can't touch yourself or pleasure yourself. I'm the only one who can do that, so you must be nice to me. Do everything I ask you to do, because without my help this will be the most frustrating encounter you will ever experience.'

The soft tones of her voice washed over him and he drowned in them. But he knew she was wrong. He was already getting pleasure out of the encounter, thank you very much, and surely that must have been obvious to her. Melissa pulled a visitor's chair from beneath his conference table and pushed it towards him. It comprised a simple chrome frame with a fabric seat, a fabric back, and no arms.

'Sit,' she ordered. 'Arms over the back.'

This, Kevin was happy to do. From this position she could clamber onto his lap, or kneel before him and take it in her mouth. Intrigued to know which she would choose, he sat straight, his legs spread, his ankles wide.

Obviously enjoying herself now, she once again took up the roll of tape and grasped one ankle. To his shock she pulled his leg outside the frame and began to bind his ankle to the back leg of the chair. He resisted faintly for a brief instant, then, almost as if she had him hypnotised, he relaxed without her needing to say a single word. His other leg followed suit on the other side, forcing him to arch upward and back into a stretched, almost kneeling posture with his thighs uncomfortably parted over the seat. But it was not all bad, for his prick jutted firmly from his groin, and the added stretch made him feel vulnerable and exposed in the whole of his nether region, and the only way she could service him now was with her mouth. He liked that thought.

He was still wallowing in anticipation as Melissa grabbed the chair and shuffled it back a little until Kevin's head and arms pressed against the wall, presumably to stop the unstable ensemble from toppling over backwards. Still fully clothed, she stood back and viewed her captive with some satisfaction. 'There, doesn't that feel nice?' she said, once again reaching to toy with his prick. When he didn't instantly answer, her head dipped to his tool and her teeth nipped at the loose flesh of his foreskin. He jerked at the unexpected pain and the erotic sensation of pleasure it sent through him. No one had ever done such a thing to him before, either. He was drowning in exciting new sensations, and it was utterly, utterly wonderful.

'Say, "yes Melissa", when I ask if it's nice. And when I've finished say, "thank you, Melissa".'

'Yes Melissa,' he whispered in absolute anticipation, his eyes never leaving hers.

She smiled in a way he didn't like too much as she opened a drawer in his desk and removed a pair of scissors. She then snipped through the single layer of fabric beneath him, and let the two severed edges hang.

He yanked against the bonds in consternation. 'What on earth are you doing? Do you realise how much these chairs cost?'

'It was in the way,' she said huskily, and knelt between his legs. One hand reached up and began to caress the small area of flesh between his anus and his balls, the other began to gently slide up and down the length of his pulsing penis. 'Is this what you want?' she cooed as he closed his eyes and sighed. 'Is this nice, Kevin?'

He gasped and forgot about the way the chrome frame was digging into his inner thighs and about how he was going to explain away the damaged seat. All he knew was that he was stretched wide and vulnerable for her skilled hands to pleasure him, and it was wonderful. She reached into his groin and separated one ball from the tightness there, and began to roll it between her fingers. It was almost painful, but exquisite.

'Oh, yes,' he gasped. 'Oh, bloody hell.' Sweat beaded his torso. It was not in his nature to lie back and take this. His hands worked convulsively behind his back, and had they not been restrained they would have reached for her, touched her, exposed her breasts. He wanted to be in control, yet being out of control was the most amazing thing he had ever experienced. He was shocked at the level of arousal it engendered in him. An arousal more painful, more vibrant than anything he had experienced in a long time.

Then his world fell apart as something tightened around his balls, bringing his wandering mind back to the present with a start. He was about to remonstrate, to say that enough was enough, when she stood up, firmly holding two ends of string which had been passed beneath the frame. These she wrapped efficiently around his torso, holding him loosely to the back of the chair, and tied off on his chest. He stared down at the knot in confusion. 'What on earth are you doing?' he asked.

She grinned, bending down to his executive case to take out some keys. 'I'm going to have a little look at your records, my hero.'

He struggled in anger for just a second, freezing almost instantly, for the slightest movement pulled his balls in a most uncomfortable manner. 'You can't do that,' he blurted. 'Those records are private, they belong to the company.'

'And who's going to stop me... you?' she smirked. 'I know they're private, that's why I'm looking at them and why I tied you up.'

His lust chilled with realisation. She was not there for him – she was using him. If looks could kill, she would have been flayed alive. 'You won't get away with this,' he threatened impotently.

'You could call for help. There must be someone in the building.' She unlocked his filing cabinets and began to browse. She was very efficient, obviously knowing exactly what she wanted and where to find it. Then, when she had a small pile of papers, she went over and unlocked the door. 'I'm just going to the photocopier. Don't go away.'

Kevin had never felt so stupid or exposed, and his penis withered as he stared at the unlocked door. He shuffled hopefully, wondering if his flaccid state would allow him to slip free of the string, but it was not to be. Horror seeped through his brain as he waited. If anyone found him like this he was finished. He'd never be such an unfaithful prat again. Oh, God, he heard heels clacking along the corridor. This was it – the end of the line.

But it was just Melissa. He didn't think he would be pleased to see her, but he was more than pleased, he was reprieved and grateful. Thank you, God. She entered briskly, put all his folders right back where they had been before and locked the drawers. He thought nothing could ever make him feel so small, so stupid, until she turned to him again and the flash of a camera made him blink and flinch. His ego totally disappeared as he saw his job and his future disappear in that one blinding moment.

Her gaze was contemptuous, her voice sarcastic. 'Not all women are bimbos, Kevin. Not all women are just itching to get into your pants. Some of us do more interesting jobs. Like industrial espionage, for instance. And arrogant suckers like you make my job very easy.' She took the scissors and advanced. He whimpered slightly as she threatened his privates with the open blades. She grinned. 'What are you supposed to say to me?'

He looked up at her vacantly, pitifully.

'Come on,' she insisted, 'you know what you have to say.'

'Th-thank you, Melissa,' he stammered.

She laughed at him, cut the string, then pulled the chair away from the wall and put the scissors in his hands, saying, 'I advise you not to drop them. It should only take you a few moments to get out of that. By then I'll be long gone. You've got two choices. You can forget about this whole incident and just hope it doesn't damage your firm – I guess the level of damage always depends on quite what the firm is hiding, don't you think? Or you can let your bosses know I've taken sensitive information through your own inability to keep your flies buttoned. But if you're unwise enough to do the latter, I will publish the photographs. I think you need to consider the options carefully, Kevin. Don't you?'

She blew him a kiss, those full pouting lips still able to make his flaccid cock twitch instinctively, and then the door closed behind her and she was gone.

Kevin bent himself furiously to the task of releasing himself, terrified of being discovered in this most undignified of positions, nothing more urgent than the need to get his clothes back on.

Yet after the panic was over, when he was driving home, eager for the comforts of his wife's stability, he knew in one thing Melissa was wrong. He didn't need to consider carefully about what he was going to do; he knew from the moment she handed him the scissors that he had no intention of saying anything to anyone about the humiliating incident.

But he did smoulder for days, with the simple wish to get his own back. If ever he saw her again, Melissa would wish she had never been born.

Chapter Four

Esther had chosen her garb over the last few weeks, partially because the black leather had a distinctive smell which made her feel good, and partially because it was what Kevin wanted. She had been very, very tentatively sounding Kevin out with some pictures in magazines, having discreetly left them open at various erotic pictures. There was the frothy kittenish appearance, the rubber, the schoolgirl and other role-play outfits, which did nothing for him. He seemed quite interested in the normal high heels, stockings and bra, but what really turned him on was the leather. Though he called the women with leather dresses and high heeled boots dominant cows, and seemed disgusted that such pictures should be in a magazine his own wife had been able to purchase from the supermarket, with her new-found wisdom, Esther watched his eyes. They betrayed him with a glint of interest. Her Kevin?

'The funny thing is, he probably doesn't realise it himself,' she told Madam Tisset, once she was over the shock.

'I don't doubt it,' the woman agreed. 'Convention and role expectations are powerful tools. They will stop the most exciting people from realising their dreams. It's only the brave or the adventurous who manage to smash the boundaries imposed by society, and choose their own lifestyle.'

'But surely that's what Kevin is doing with these other women?'

'No, dear, he's doing what men all through life have been doing. He's simply cheating on you. He might think that being with other women is risqué, yet when he's with them, the sex itself is no better than he could have with you if he would only open up a bit and discuss what he wants.'

'I didn't realise he had those sort of sexual fantasies until I started coming here,' Esther said glumly.

'My dear, don't you have any?' Esther's blush was a dead give-away, but she carried on kindly. 'Everyone does, you know, but for most people they stay in the mind, never to see the light of day, which is a great shame. Imagination is the very essence of good sex – that and the ability to enjoy what you're doing. Give me a word to describe the sex you have with Kevin.'

Esther thought about it. 'It's nice enough,' she said hesitantly, for Kevin was a considerate and competent lover.

'"Nice enough". You see what I mean? If someone said my dress was "nice enough" I'd want to hit them. I want them to say: "stylish, different, exciting" – not just "nice enough". Nice is just not enough to keep you over sixty years of marriage. Have you ever wondered why such a lot of people divorce at around forty or so, when their children begin to leave home? It's because they're bored with each other. And that's what society has done to them.'

'Were you ever married?' Esther asked.

'Me? No, no. I was never the marrying type. No way I could ever be faithful to just one man. I love the lot of them. Besides, I can't stand children.' She shuddered dramatically at the awful prospect. 'Now, dear, I've got someone for you to meet.' She stood up and opened the door into a small dark cupboard which was furnished with nothing but a chair, and on that chair sat a man, hands on thighs, waiting to be commanded. 'You can come out, now,' she said. 'Esther, this is Ben. Ben is going to help us with our lessons today. Aren't you, Ben?'

'Yes, Madam Tisset.'

Esther gazed with astonishment at the positively huge young man who beamed at her. He was built like a weightlifter, his chest beaded with muscles, his thighs like tree trunks. Yet he was dressed like something out of a fantasy movie, in tiny leather shorts and an assortment which seemed to be nothing more than straps and buckles covered in patterns of studs. As her gaze slipped down she blushed furiously, realising that his penis was sticking out of the shorts through a hole obviously designed for that purpose.

Madam Tisset put her hands on her hips. 'Esther, you must stop doing that.'

'What?' she said, guilty at being caught looking.

'Blushing. That is partially what today is about. By the end of the day there will be nothing you haven't seen and done to our slave here. So there will be nothing left for you to blush about.'

'Slave?'

'You can tie him up, beat him, stick things in him. And if he pleases you, you can make him come at the end of the session,' she added as an afterthought.

'Anything which pleases,' Ben said happily.

'Goodness. I don't know – I mean, wouldn't I be as bad as Kevin if I did such things?'

Madam Tisset patted her shoulder kindly. 'You don't have sex with him, dear. Just beat him around a little. Get it out of your system. Show him who's boss. Now go and get dressed while I get him ready, and then we can get on.'

While donning the leather gear, Esther sipped at the glass of wine Madam Tisset had left there for her. She was needing the wine less these days, but today was rather different. She'd never had a real live slave to abuse before, and the prospect was a bit daunting, as well as exciting. She wondered what she could do to him, how far he would let her go. She reflected that had this happened a few months back she would have run a mile, and yet here she was, ready to have a go. Not that she had been able to take any of her new-found confidence home yet. In spite of everything, she still shied away from instigating any games with Kevin because she knew with chilling certainty that she was going to have to play her cards right, and that she was not ready for such a confrontation. Even so, she was seeing her husband with new eyes these days. Her own sense of inadequacy and her awe for his wonderful male superiority was wearing a bit thin. She now knew his tiredness for what it was, and smelled the scent of other women on him. It was at that point that any residual feelings of betrayal she might have felt in coming to these sessions finally fled. The only person entitled to abuse her husband, she decided firmly at that moment, was herself. Soon enough she would make sure of that.

'Are you ready, Esther, dear?'

Madam Tisset wandered in wearing her own chosen outfit; a very slinky red rubber dress. A few weeks ago Esther would have thought her a sad woman, but now she treated the older lady with respect, combined with a surprising amount of real affection. Once, if anyone had hinted she might ever become friendly with a self-confessed whore, she would have been most indignant. But not now.

'Yes, I'm ready,' she said.

'Right. The first rule of keeping a slave is discipline. It's a bit like having a dog. You have to be firm to be kind. The slave must always know what is expected, because if he's confused he can become unhappy with his position. Now, for the most part we can keep him chained up – there are various interesting positions – or in that cage over there when he's not required. I prefer them chained, myself, because they have a certain decorative quality. I also like to keep them gagged to stop them from inadvertently irritating me with silly questions and demands, but you can always remove it if you're in need of some really serious grovelling.'

Esther's giggle was part shock, part amusement, part excitement. Ben now stood in a stretched star in the middle of the large room, his wrists chained to a spreader above his head, his ankles locked into a spreader attached to the floor. His mouth was propped open by a rubber bit.

'Now, dear,' Madam Tisset went on, 'he's all yours... aren't you, Ben?'

Ben nodded, and mumbled something.

'What did he say?'

'Thank you, Madam. Slaves are grateful to be noticed,

whether you wish to speak to them or simply abuse them. And if they forget, then you must remind them in such a way it doesn't happen again. Slaves must never be allowed to forget their manners.'

Esther stood hesitantly, wondering what she should do, and Madam Tisset tut-tutted. 'You've got the costume on, girl. Become it! Do what you want. Examine him. See what he's made of. Take his pants off and have a good look at his penis. I doubt you've ever looked at Kevin's that closely, have you? Once you know what you're dealing with you can stop being afraid of it. It's not magic the way his silly tool gets big, it's blood pressure, and the biggest weapon you have is knowing how to control his valves. Once you've done that, the next thing to learn is where his pleasure centres are. They're his weak points. With that knowledge you will never feel small again. Now, go ahead.'

Not feeling at all dominant, Esther reluctantly stepped forward, and once again Madam Tisset took charge. She spread her hands out and rubbed them all over the chained man's torso and thighs as though she was rubbing down a horse. 'Like this, dear, now join in. Even this surface rubbing has a reason. You see, it brings tiny blood vessels to the surface, makes everything more sensitive, so when you hit him later it's far more effective.'

Growing more confident as time went on, Esther smoothed her hands firmly across Ben's hard chest, twiddled his nipples firmly, then ran her hands down to the top of his shorts, thinking how much hairier he was than Kevin. She rubbed her hands up and down his hard thighs, slipping a finger under the rim where the shorts tightly encompassed his flesh. Then she walked around him and, getting more familiar, ground herself against the tiny buttocks to make her own leather garb creak against her, creating strange erotic sensations to flood her middle. After a while Esther found that touching the man all over when he could neither reciprocate or argue made him less of a human being, more of an object to be played with and manipulated.

She grew braver, stronger. Then she ran her fingers up his tapered back, along the ridges of muscle on his broad shoulders, felt the raised blood vessels pulsing under her hands. Walking around the front once more, she slid both hands up the thickness of his neck, pushed her fingers into the wiry mass of his hair and pulled her thumbs down over his cheeks, sliding them under the web of straps that held the bit in place. Then she went one step further and fed a finger into his mouth above the bit, pushing his tongue this way and that. He groaned, and she realised with shock that the penis was no longer flaccid. She had made the man rampant. Was it really that easy?

When she made love with Kevin she sometimes had to knead him into fullness before he could make love to her. She didn't like having to do that, it was as if he wasn't really interested in her as a woman, that simply being there wasn't enough to make him fancy her. She now knew she was right and was slightly saddened that she might have gone for the rest of her life without realising this simple fact.

But why was this man so rampant when she was touching anything except his penis? Then the penny dropped. Anticipation. Oh, goodness. The answer had been there all along. All the years of her marriage she'd been trying to milk Kevin like a cow, when what he needed was other stimuli. Yet why hadn't he told her that? It was this Victorian double standard at work again, she realised. One thing for the whore, but the wife was supposed to lie back in the dark and think of England. It wasn't really fair, was it?

But one thing that did happen, with all that touching and with the fellow, big as he was, chained up like that, she realised she felt nothing but superiority over him. He was vastly her superior in the muscle department alone, but at that moment she was the boss. She could do to him whatever she wanted. Now she wanted to see him all.

She discovered the shorts were held in place by a buckle on each hip. She released them one by one, only to discover the shorts held more surprises than the man's body alone. In the front his balls were encased in another tight leather pouch, which she had to release, and at the back a dildo slid out of his anus when she pulled them from him.

She made a tiny noise of shock and looked over at Madam Tisset, who was now lounging in a torture chair with her legs crossed. 'Does he enjoy stuff like that?' she asked, indicating the shorts.

'The more uncomfortable you make his privates, the more he can't take his mind off them. And if it begins to hurt, so much the better. You see, pain is as near to pleasure as you can get. The slave will get more pleasure from his erogenous zones being respectively constricted, forced apart or beaten, as he will from the final act of ejaculation. The trick is to make him feel a whole multitude of emotions, ones he cannot control or escape from or assist in, hence the immobilisation. Over the session these will amalgamate into a single massive experience which his pea-brain will later tell him he has enjoyed.'

She uncurled from her seat. 'Right, now you're relaxed about it all, we'll look at the various sexual aids. To start with we'll go through the insertion tools, go on to the constriction devices – do find out which ones excite you, never mind what he likes at this moment, he's there to please you, no more – and once you've done that you can try out the paddles and whips.'

'But what if I hurt him?'

'I'll add it to his bill. Right, Ben?'

Ben nodded and mumbled again.

Esther was slightly shocked. 'But I thought I was going to have to pay *him*.'

'Good God, no,' Madam Tisset scoffed. 'He's not getting all this for free. What do you think I am, a charitable institution? Now, have a look at these.' She pulled out a drawer full of stainless steel tools which would have done justice to a surgeon.

After some instruction, and with a little trepidation, Esther practised. She took the flaccid penis into her hand and tentatively began to insert one of the long slender tools. Ben's whole body tensed and quivered as she found the entrance to his urethra and slid the tool in. There was a small groan from behind the gag. She moved the probe around, prodding and pulling so the curved end touched various places inside him. He tensed, and the penis became huge.

'Is that right?' she asked uncertainly.

He nodded, gasping and shuddering, and a small dribble

of liquid slid over her fingers.

'After a while that can be quite painful. Especially if you make him drink lots of water and instruct him to hold it,' Madam Tisset said, pouring herself a cup of tea. 'They can find that quite nice. And that tube there is quite a good one. If you push that in, then use the bulb to pressurise it, you can stop them from peeing at all until you release it. They use that in hospitals for people with incontinence. It takes a bit of practice to get it in, though, so perhaps we should leave it until later.'

'And this?' Esther asked, becoming more intrigued by the array of implements.

'Oh, that one does the same thing at the rear end. You can blow it up like a balloon inside him, cramp his bowels up something lovely. Go on, have a try. You might need to use some lubricant – the finger is the best way of doing that. I've already flushed him out, given him an enema, so he's not going to do anything nasty. Now, I've got to go and make some calls to clients. Get on and enjoy yourself, and just call if you need me. That's an impressive erection you've got there,' she added admiringly.

Esther found herself distanced from reality. She was in a room where a man she had never seen before was strung up in chains for her pleasure. Not only had he allowed it voluntarily, but he was paying for it. Madam Tisset was talking about him as if he was a piece of meat, and she, herself, was sticking things in his private places, which he seemed to be enjoying immensely. It made her feel very powerful and important.

She lubricated his anus as Madam Tisset had told her, and pushed the plug in. There was a faint resistance before it was sucked into place. She then proceeded to blow it up. At the first few pumps there was no reaction, then he made gasping noises, then he made groaning noises. When he made little strangled noises in his throat and began to convulse against the chains she thought she had gone far enough, so released the pressure and began all over again. It was a bit like winding up a toy and watching it go.

When Madam Tisset came back in a while later, Ben was covered in a sheen of sweat, his balls sported a weight of rather impressive size, and Esther was beating his buttocks with a short cat-o'-nine-tails made of rubber. His penis was pendulous and leaking, and every so often the tips of the whip would catch the back of his balls and send him writhing.

'Very good,' Madam Tisset complimented. 'Of course, the one thing that would make this all slightly more exciting for him would be to put a blindfold on him. Then he would have no idea where the next lash will fall. If he can't anticipate, he can't stop himself from reacting. But that's enough for now, dearie. Ben has to go to work in a minute, so do you want to have a go at finishing him off, or shall I do it?'

'How would he want it to be done?' Esther said hesitantly.

'My dear, it doesn't matter what the slave wants. That's not what this is all about. You're the mistress here. You're supposed to be doing what *you* want. Have you enjoyed yourself? Has it made you feel exceedingly randy, so that you want to go home and leap on Kevin?'

'Yes,' Esther said with feeling. 'I feel all wound up and nowhere to go.'

'Excellent. Then finish him off, like this – then let him down and send him to me in the office when he's showered.'

Esther used her hand as Madam Tisset had shown her.

'Thank you, Madam,' he gasped as she took the gag out of his mouth. 'Can I visit you again, please? You're very good.'

And so the self-confidence lessons progressed.

Chapter Five

Several weeks later Kevin arrived home on a Sunday evening to greet Esther with a quick kiss and a large sigh. 'Hello, darling. Sorry I'm later than expected. It's been the most trying week. Working all hours, staying at that damned hotel all weekend for the conference.'

'You poor dear,' Esther said sympathetically. 'Perhaps it's time you had a little holiday. Anyway, you're home now. Come and have your dinner. I've only been keeping it warm for an hour or so.'

He sniffed appreciatively and thought how nice it was to have plain English cooking after the excessively rich food in the hotel. 'Roast beef, just like mother made. Essie, honey, you're a wonder!'

'Slip your shoes off, sit down and have a glass of wine, darling. You must be absolutely knackered. You've been working far too hard lately, you know. You're hardly ever here.'

'Honey, you're a wonderful little wife, you know that?' he said, relaxing under her sensitive ministrations, and swirling the pale liquid around in the glass before throwing it down in one. 'I knew I was on to a good thing when I met you.'

'I try to be a good little wife,' she said dutifully, and knelt on the floor to massage his feet. 'I'm learning new things all the time.'

'Aah,' Kevin sighed, stretching luxuriously, not hearing the extra sugar in his wife's tone. 'Is this part of what you learned at those classes?'

'Uh-huh. This and much, much more.'

He patted her head absently. Esther smiled secretively, and rose to serve the dinner.

'Have you been shopping, Essie, honey? Did you manage to get me some new shirts?'

'Sorry, darling, I was busy sorting out the garage. You know I've been meaning to do it for months. I'll get your shirts tomorrow. I'm intending to go shopping.'

'Find anything interesting in the garage?'

'An awful lot of rubbish and an army of spiders.'

Kevin shuddered. He had a morbid fear of spiders, and if anything was calculated to keep him out of the garage, that was. If Esther wanted him to help out in there, no way. 'What are you cleaning the garage out for, anyway?'

'I was thinking of turning it into a sort of utility room. You know we never bother to put the car in there, so we won't miss it.'

'Won't that cost a lot?'

'Apart from scrubbing it from head to toe, a lick of paint is all it needs, and I can do that myself. It'll be well worth the effort and will free up some kitchen space, make it easier for me to iron your shirts.'

He glanced up and thought for a fleeting moment that Esther's tone had a slightly sarcastic note to it, but realised he must be mistaken; she wore her normal placid expression. Somehow, before they were married, she had been stronger, had more vitality. He couldn't help wondering where that had all gone. Still, one couldn't have everything. He grinned to himself; at least, not at home. Cleaning up the garage was a good idea; it kept Esther busy if nothing else, and the busier she was, the less she was likely to sit around and worry about where he was. He turned his attention to the perfectly roasted, if rather dry, potatoes. Yep, she was a good little wife all right.

When he'd finished eating he slouched into the lounge, dropped into his favourite chair, stretched his legs, and interlocked his fingers behind his head. He smiled at Esther. 'You know, it's at times like this I really know how lucky I am to have you.'

As Kevin wallowed in complacency, Esther glanced around the neat room and suddenly realised how sterile it all seemed. There was nothing of her here. Nothing of Kevin, either, when it came down to it. Just a perfect show home for when people called. Not that they very often did. He had few friends at work, and she seemed to have drifted from hers over the years.

She had been feeling slightly fainthearted during the day, thinking that perhaps her plans were a bit drastic, but found her courage buoyed by the thought that she was saving their marriage. Another year or so down the line and it would simply be too late; there would be nothing left to save. She fetched his glass and flicked the television on.

'Here, have some more wine and watch the match while I wash up. I recorded it for you, as you've been working so hard lately.'

'You did? Honey, that was so thoughtful.' Recollecting what he had actually been doing, and knowing how much she hated football, he had the grace to look slightly guilty, but what the hell. It was nice to be pampered, and it was time he called it a day with Alicia; she really couldn't excite him any more.

Esther looked back around the door, 'Oh, I'm just going to pop over to Jenny's for coffee. I promised her I'd go round for a chat, and just forgot about the time.'

'That's fine, honey. See you later.'

From the kitchen Esther watched Kevin through the open door. He really was a fine specimen by anybody's standards. Even now she recalled the thrill of attraction that gripped her when she'd first met him, and somehow he had grown even more sexy in the last couple of years. And she knew she was special to him; she had seen that cold arrogance with which he treated others, and thanked God it wasn't ever directed at her. She knew he could be a right bastard with people he didn't like very much. But whatever he was like at work, when he was impressing the directors or wangling deals out of others, at home he was getting set in his ways, complacent as an old sofa.

She felt her anger building at the sudden thought of that rather pretty young thing called Chrissie something-or-other who had accosted her at the business function. It didn't take much imagination to know what she and Kevin had been to each other at some time. Yet whatever that woman now had against Kevin, Esther didn't care any more. Madam Tisset's business card had been given to her in the true spirit of spite, but it wasn't going to wreck her marriage, it was going to save it, even if the manner of achieving it was going to be one hell of a shock to dear Kevin. Esther hummed as she washed up, and found herself getting very excited.

Twenty minutes later, hands on hips, she surveyed her dearly beloved. Kevin would have been shocked at the expression on her face – had he been awake to see it. The potion Madam Tisset had given her had worked a treat. He was lolling back in the chair, arms draped over the edges, television forgotten, and the empty wine glass on the floor beneath his hand. Esther picked it up. 'Naughty boy,' she said softly, seeing the little damp patch of wine on the carpet. 'Madam is going to have to punish you for that.'

Kevin felt hands pulling at his shirt. He tried to wake himself from the strangest lethargy he had ever felt, but could not. Dimly he heard a voice he had never heard before, one filled with the harsh ring of authority.

'Don't try to speak, slave, just listen and obey my voice. You've been a naughty boy, gadding about with lots of other women, and your mistress is going to put a stop to all that, do you hear? Now, push yourself on to your feet. Come on! Get on with it, I can't lift you on my own!'

Kevin vaguely recognised the voice of authority, and made an effort to assist, not that he was aware of what he did. Esther had learned how to inflect her voice with just the quality that would make a man jump to her bidding; Madam had been quite thorough in her teachings.

Slowly he gained his feet, but could not quite focus his mind. His eyes wouldn't quite seem to open, but he felt himself clamber into a car, and heard the engine cough into life. The motion of the car began to send him to sleep. Bloody hell, he was tired. She was right, whoever she was; he really should have more respect for Esther, only he just couldn't seem to stop himself going after the other women. It was the excitement factor. Damn, he couldn't think straight. What was the matter with him? He didn't know where he was or where he was going, and couldn't recall which of his flings this was, but if she thought he was going to get it up tonight, she was going to be very disappointed; he needed to sleep.

The car stopped. Esther was alarmed when he began to snore. 'Not yet,' she snapped. 'Stand up! No, don't fall. Move forward! That's right. Hang in there! Keep moving. Two more steps. Good boy.'

Then his knees began to buckle. 'Can't stand any more,' he slurred.

'You can sit down now. Gently does it. There, the bed is behind you.'

He flopped thankfully onto the softness of his bed. The voice was familiar somehow, yet he couldn't place it at all. It was most confusing, yet rather nice, in a way. The voice was authoritative, not allowing him to lie down, and he felt like a child again, being mothered. He felt gentle hands creep up his front, undoing his shirt button by button. He realised she was undressing him. Putting him to bed. Hands caressed the hairs on his chest. Vaguely interested, he tried to move his arms, but they were like lumps of iron glued to his sides.

'Lean forward. Just a bit, whoa, not too far...' The shirt slid down over his shoulders and was gone. 'Now you can lie down.' He wavered thankfully and slumped onto his back. She lifted his feet, twisted his legs onto the bed, took his shoes off. Then her hands crept to his trousers, unbuckled his belt, unhooked the clasp. His hips moved fractionally in response to the feather-light touch of the zipper sliding down, and there was a faint stirring of interest from between his legs. But no – it didn't want to play again so soon. He vaguely recalled fucking Alicia, but what the hell had happened after that? He couldn't recall, but damn it felt good.

'I don't think I can...' he tried to say, perturbed by his own inability. 'Too tired...'

'No bother,' the woman whispered in a seductive voice. 'You don't need to do anything. Just relax, honey-bun. We'll do things later. Now, just lift your hips for me.'

Honey-bun? Who the hell would call him honey-bun? The name caused a brief flutter of irritation, then he was being moved again. His trousers slid down over his feet and were gone. His pants went the same way. Then, as he lay there on the bed in this strange and unusual lethargy, to his surprise he began to have an erotic dream. He dreamed that soft hands upon his body were wrapping leather straps around his wrists and stretching his arms high, to almost unbearable tightness, and buckling them firmly to the bedhead. Chest expanded, feet tingling with suspense, he pulled at the bonds, but they were firm.

A soft smile formed. He sank deeper into sleep. Soft leather encompassed his ankles and his legs were parted and secured. He moaned and writhed with severe sensual pleasure as his dream woman tethered him fast for her pleasure. Oh boy, what a dream. Through his subconscious a faint embarrassment filtered, diminished the pleasure slightly. Blimey, what would Esther think of him if she knew? Still, there was no harm in dreaming, and what she didn't know couldn't... oh *yes*, hands were fondling him.

His strained awareness was sucked instantly to that flaccid lump of flesh between his legs.

Despite his lethargy and his inability to comprehend what had caused the strange dream, he felt his penis begin to expand, to fill those soft hands. It was the hands of an expert – the hands of a whore. Damn! but she knew where to rub. His penis got bigger and bigger, it throbbed, ached, swelled gloriously. She held his penis away from his navel with one firm hand, softly drew back the foreskin with the other, and began to make small circular motions with the palm of her hand on the tip of his throbbing knob.

'Oh, baby,' he whispered. 'Oh, baby, do it to me, baby.' His imagination worked overtime. He thought of that waitress with big tits and imagined it was her sitting over him, fondling him, leaning her melon-sized boobs in his face, lifting her tiny skirt with nothing underneath... 'Do it,' he whispered. 'I'm ready. Do it to me, baby.'

But to his irritation the hands left him and he gradually wilted. He struggled to open his eyes, but the dream had him locked in darkness. He wasn't sure whether his eyes were open or not, and although the strange lethargy began to fade and the cotton wool seemed to recede from his brain, he still found himself stretched unnaturally tightly in bonds which were surprisingly real. Suddenly frightened, his erection disappeared absolute. He tried desperately to wake himself, but he could not. Drifting in and out of sleep for a while, Kevin wasn't sure at what point he became sure he was not dreaming. The dream had long ago lost its drive, lost its eroticism, and he wanted out of it, only it wouldn't let go.

Finally he woke up fully to the understanding that he

was stretched out naked, strapped in a star shape on a metal bed by restraints made of thick padded leather which felt horribly serious. His penis had shrivelled completely. He whimpered. What if someone came and found him like this?

His new consciousness told him he must have been drugged, and was no longer under the influence of whatever he'd been given. But somewhere in the back of his mind he recalled Esther making him a drink and going out. After that he had climbed in a car with some woman, but it was all so vague. Where the hell was he? He peered, but the darkness didn't diminish. It wasn't the darkness of night, it was simply the darkness of a place without light. A place with locks on the doors, with leather straps holding him firmly in place. He struggled, panicked by the unknown quantity of his situation, and to add to his discomfort, he was busting for a pee.

What the hell was going on? Where was Esther? Did she realise he was gone? Was she even now calling the police? He imagined her at home, distraught, wondering where he was.

His need to pee grew, and his fear grew. What did they want with him? What did *who* want with him? In the darkness he gyrated his wrists in the cuffs. They were tough, padded, and immovable. He shifted. Got his hands around stout chains. Was he a man, or what? So, he'd break the fucking bed. He pulled with all his not inconsiderable strength. He yanked, he pulled, he swore. Nothing gave. Nothing moved. He stopped, panted, and there was only one thing left to do.

'Help?'

It sounded pitiful, even to his ears, and his next cry was louder. 'Help!'

Eventually his voice grew hoarse with calling, but no one came. Finally, having no choice, he allowed his aching muscles to relax and with a long sigh of satisfaction, relieved himself on the bed. It was a momentary relief followed by an even greater feeling of horror. What if someone came now and found him lying in a pool of his own urine?

At long last a key grated in the lock. The door opened. The light was blinding. Kevin's eyes automatically shut, but not so soon that the woman's form was not burned with shocking intensity into his mind. He caught a fleeting image of thrusting bosom and rounded hips encased in something form-huggingly tight – something black with laces. She was a dark shadow sharply outlined in yellow light; she had an athletic body, and though she was wearing a mask he knew with absolute certainty that he had never met her in his life.

Yet he'd seen pictures of women like that before, and the word that instantly came to mind was dominatrix.

Despite his furious and panic-stricken attempts to stop the woman, she leaned over and encased his head in a mesh of straps that held a very efficient blindfold in place.

The hands tested their work, and found it satisfactory. He writhed with fury in his bonds. 'Who are you?' he shrieked. 'What the fuck are you doing? Let me up before I kill you, you bitch!'

He stopped yelling. There was no answer, but she moved. His ears homed in on soft sounds to his left. 'Who the fuck are you? What do you want with me?'

The woman's voice was as he had expected, almost a whisper, low and husky. 'I want you, slave,' she informed him.

He pulled angrily at the bonds, feeling scared, incredibly stupid and, in spite of himself, flattered. 'Well you can't have me! Now let me up, you bitch!'

There was the fleeting hint of a whistle, and he screamed as pain bit across his upper thighs. 'Quiet, slave,' she said softly.

Kevin whimpered slightly, shocked into near-silence by the throbbing pain. She hit him! The bitch had actually hit him! There was a long silence while he digested this amazing fact. 'Why...'

'Shhhh...'

He bit his lip, hearing a threat in the soft sound.

He felt the sheet, or something, being pulled from underneath him. He was wiped like a baby, and then heard the sound of running water. 'Now lift your hips,' she commanded.

'What're you doing?'

A faint chuckle. 'Nothing terrible. I'm just going to clean you up. I need to put a towel under you so you don't mess my sheets.'

Kevin scowled and didn't oblige. She could go to hell. He would enjoy pissing on her sheets, dammit. The unknown woman, however, merely took a handful of his exposed sexual organs and lifted. She had sharp nails. Up he arched, gasping with shock.

'What you have to realise, slave,' she said informatively in her low voice, as she wound a warm soapy flannel between his legs, 'is that I own you. You do not have a name. You have no identity at all except in that you have to please me. And what you have to learn quickly,' she purred, 'is how to please me well.'

'Fuck you!' he snapped.

'Exactly,' she replied, giving him a congratulatory pat.

'What?'

'Fuck me. But so that it pleases me, not you. That little lump of flesh,' she flicked his penis disparagingly, 'belongs to me. As does the whole of this fine body. I may do with it what I will, and it will obey me.' Her breath purred on the words, and her nails raked softly and seductively down the length of his tense thigh muscles.

'I'm Kevin Mellinton, not anybody's bloody slave, and I want out of here or I'll call the police,' he yelled.

'You're a sex slave, here to serve faithfully until the day you die.'

'I won't!'

'Won't you?'

'You can't make me.'

'Can't I?'

Kevin tensed, hearing movement, and discovered to his horror that he was afraid of her as he had never in his life before been afraid of anyone, let alone a woman. He felt the bed sag slightly as she climbed over him and knelt astride his body, knees outside his hips, feet inside his thighs. Everything went tight with panic. He couldn't breath. Then he gasped as a cool trickle of liquid slid unexpectedly onto his chest and she began to rub it in.

Very, very gently, she traced circles around his tense chest muscles, merely spreading the oil. Then she kneaded, pushed, and rubbed them into submission with slick fingers. She rolled his nipples between her fingertips, then worked her way downward until she had covered every exposed area, and in spite of himself he knew he was enjoying the experience, that his body was tuning in to her sexuality; relaxing outwardly, but pulsing deep inside with vibrant sexual need. As she leaned over his body with those expert and strong fingers that danced so erotically, he felt the warmth of her breath across his mouth. Then she slid forward to nuzzle him beneath his chin, up the side of his face, in his ear. Oh, the soft weight of her breast hung against his sensitised skin, moving the hairs of his chest with the subtlety of a summer's breeze.

His penis swelled. It was impossible to stop it. He groaned with annoyance, pleasure, fear, and anger at her easy manipulation of him, but when his rising prick encountered softness, wetness and warmth, it hardened instantly into a thrusting tool.

She didn't lower herself onto him, though. She teased, and he felt the contractions of her vagina fluctuate against the tip of his penis then slide away again and again. 'Oh, God,' he said hoarsely. 'If you're going to do it, bloody-well do it! Don't just piss about!'

'I am doing it,' she replied softly. He groaned. 'I'm pleasing myself. You're just the slave upon which I'm choosing to do it.' He felt her strong thigh muscles come into play again, and he slid out of her once more. She began to rub herself up and down the base of his rampant penis giving him no satisfaction whatsoever, and for the first time in his sexual career, he realised that achievement of his orgasm was not first and foremost in his partner's mind. She stretched out, her feet separated and slid down the length of his stretched legs, and he felt her doing press-ups over his rampant sex while her lips brushed and rubbed at various body parts; his lips, his chin and ears, and his nipples.

Faster and faster she went, rubbing herself forward and backward until he was nearly crying with the strange, erotic sensations she was producing. Then with a groan, she came. Kevin felt the small pulse of her orgasm against his balls. He'd never felt that before. Esther never did that. Alicia never did that; nor Jeannie, nor Rose, nor Suzanne... the list was endless, his memories tortured. Had they all been faking? With a blinding flash of understanding, he realised he had never made a woman come in his life.

His need overtook him. He groaned. The unknown woman climbed from him, sated. He moved, writhed, begged without words for her to take him in her hands and finish the job. She couldn't leave him like this...

He sensed she was watching.

'Say it,' she said softly.

No, he couldn't. He'd never beg!

'Say it. Ask me. Beg me.'

He groaned weakly. His penis was throbbing, and if it wasn't stimulated he knew his erection would merely melt away of its own accord, but even if it did, his need to come would remain an urgent compulsion deep inside his brain, and wouldn't disappear until it had been consummated.

'I'll say it one more time,' she warned. 'Then I'll go.'

'Please!' he gasped.

Strong fingers wrapped around him, lifted, milked

briefly, and in an instant he shot his load into the cup of her hand. 'Now what do you say?' the seductive voice persisted.

'Bastard!' he muttered. If she thought he was going to say thank you... God, he'd never said thank you before in his life! They always said it to him. Except that Michelle bitch, and this wasn't her, he'd swear.

She walked away. He heard the running of water, and his normal icy composure returned.

He said sarcastically, 'If you've quite finished, you can let me up now.'

She responded with a soft chuckle. 'Why, slave, you have such a lot to learn. I've hardly started. Be kind to yourself. Thank me for this lesson.'

A cold shiver ran down his spine. 'Fuck you,' he growled.

'If you don't do it voluntarily, I will force it out of you.'

'Bitch! Let me up!'

'I'm sorry, I can't do that. I enjoyed myself, and I want to do it again, and again, and again. But you have to learn to appreciate the quality time I'm giving you. You must learn to be grateful.'

'I don't want to be grateful,' he hissed. 'I've got a wife. I have to go home.'

Her voice was suddenly harsh. 'You don't normally care about that, so why should I?'

'But...' how much did she know about him? 'Please? Please let me up.'

'I like it when you say please.' Her voice dropped a notch. 'Say please again.'

The false sugar melted from his voice. 'Let me up you

fucking bitch!' he snarled.

'Don't scream at me, slave.'

'I'm not anybody's slave!'

'You are mine.'

He screamed as loud as he could. 'Help! Help! Rape! Murder!' He stopped and listened, hoping for help, expecting retribution, but all he heard was a soft laugh. His head followed the sound of her as she walked right around him.

'The room is soundproofed, slave. No one can help you. You're mine to do with as I please. You will wait here at my pleasure, and you will pleasure me whenever I choose. I can make you do it, you know I can. But if you're a good boy, and if you please me really, really well,' her low laughter made his skin crawl, 'I might keep you for ever and ever and ever.'

With those parting words he felt the draft of a door opening and the soft thud of its closing as she left him chained to the bed, a male rubber doll with no other reason for his existence than waiting on her pleasure. And that waiting seemed to stretch into eternity. His thoughts buzzed around the women he had been with, Esther, his work, his home, and back to whoever had him here now. He feared that unless he escaped, life as he knew it was probably over.

The next time she came into the room Kevin could only listen. He heard the door open and close. He heard the click of a switch, but not the faintest hint of light trickled through his blindfold.

'Who are you?' he asked again, tensing with unease.

'You may call me Mistress,' she said.

'Like hell.' There was silence for a moment. 'I'm hungry.'

'Well you can just stay that way until you do something to earn your food.'

He pulled with frustration at his restraints. 'I can't do anything like this.' His voice softened, wheedled. 'Let me up and I'll please you. I know how to please a woman. I can please you. I know all the places to touch...'

'I doubt that,' she said acerbically.

For a fleeting second he wondered where he'd heard that voice before, then teeth closed on his right nipple and he screamed, forgetting everything except the excruciating pain. She bit, ground her teeth together on him, and a hand slid down his stomach, over his penis and balls, between his legs, and a finger wormed into his anus. He spasmed violently at the intrusion, but his penis flickered defiantly into life. He whimpered, tried to thrust the finger out, and farted.

The indignity of it!

He gasped on a threat and a prayer as her questing tongue roamed across his chest, long strokes licking, drawing back, and licking again. He tensed with anticipation, but could do nothing to forestall the agony as she bit into the other nipple with sharp teeth. He heard her growl with pleasure deep in her throat as her teeth ground upon his throbbing flesh. 'Oh no,' he cried. 'Help me!'

But her hands worked their subtle magic on his flesh, and as her finger slid in and out of his protesting anus, so his balls tightened and his penis became engorged with the shameful pleasure of it. And once again she was able to ease herself down upon him and bring herself to the height of orgasm whether he would or no.

He felt the pulse of her orgasm wrap around him and he whimpered slightly as she paused, gasping, assuming she had finished with him. Yet she remained poised over him. 'Is that nice, slave?' she whispered.

'Yes... oh yes,' he whispered back.

'Shall I stop? Do you want me to go away?'

'No... no, don't stop, please...'

'Mistress,' she prompted.

'Mistress,' he gasped. 'Don't stop.' And then he heard her chuckle at his capitulation.

She rode him expertly, bringing him to the peak of ecstasy time and time again, pausing when his need grew too great, and then sinking softly down upon an erection more tender, more vibrant than he had ever had before. Each time he felt his orgasm coming she slowed, paused, allowed him to hold his seed. Now she moved for his satisfaction alone, for she had already come. When he could hold himself no longer he cried out, and she pressed herself down on him hard so that he came deep within her, felt her grind against his painful ejaculation, and she didn't move or say a word until the last flush had faded from his body. Then she leaned forward and kissed him tenderly. To his surprise, he kissed her back, running his tongue around her even teeth, savouring the fresh toothpaste taste of her. 'You're beautiful,' he whispered sincerely.

'And you're mine,' she said softly back.

There was a pause. 'You can't keep me here,' he told her. 'My wife will worry. I'll lose my job...'

'You've got no choice,' she told him, removing herself

from his body. 'You're my prisoner, my sexual partner, my slave, unless I choose to let you go.'

'But why me?' he said in dismay. 'Why do you want to ruin my life?'

'I don't want to ruin it,' she told him enigmatically. 'I want to make it better. Believe me, you are just the shell of the man you could become. That's why I picked you out of all the others, because you have potential. Presently you're neither a good lover, nor successful at work. But if you learn well, my slave, by the time I have finished with you, you can be both. And you'll learn to be satisfied with no woman except me.'

He groaned at the possessive purr he heard in the back of her throat. 'I have a life to return to... a wife...'

'Your wife is nothing to you, I've seen that. Don't think about her any more. Just think about me. Without me you're nothing, little man. But if you serve me well, you'll be rewarded for your labours, believe me.'

'Just let me go,' he pleaded.

He felt the soft touch of lips upon his. 'That, I may never do.'

This time, when she left, Kevin was filled with anguish. It was all very well having the odd fling, but he had never wanted the same woman more than a few times, apart from Esther. It was funny how once you'd had it with a woman it just became a routine. A chore, almost. It was a good job wives had so little sex drive. It would kill a man if they were all like this one – this Madam... this dominatrix.

But how could he ever go back to his wife now? How could he go back to his old life, his old confidence, knowing that some woman had kept him bound at her pleasure? He felt such an idiot. Yet a small betraying spark of excitement reminded him he had never felt so satiated in his life.

Bloody hell, what a woman!

He heard water running, and tested his bonds with fainthearted tugs, as he twisted his head to listen. 'What are you doing?' he called.

'I'm washing. I like to wash after sex.'

'Then what are you going to do?'

'I am going to go and get on with my work.'

He was vaguely annoyed. 'And what am I supposed to do?'

'The only thing you can do. Wait for me.'

He pulled at his bonds with more effort. 'If I could get my hands free I'd kill you for this, you bitch.'

'Enjoy thinking about it, slave, because that's all you can do.'

He heard a smile in her voice as she left. 'What about me?' he roared. 'I want to wash. I want to piss. I want to move. I'm hungry, dammit!'

The door closed behind the mystery woman.

The euphoria of that exquisite fuck began to wear off. 'Hell and damnation,' Kevin cursed. 'If ever a man has had an erotic dream, this is probably it. But it's not funny,' he yelled, in case she was listening. 'It's not bloody funny at all! I've had enough!'

He had no idea of the passing of time. He could only tell that his hunger had become an encompassing ache.

He began to think of his evenings at home with Esther. The way they had sat in silence through the police serials he enjoyed. The way she had quietly and calmly cleaned up around him before they went to bed. The way she had been so infuriatingly accommodating to his needs, making herself available; on her back without comment, like a receptacle placidly waiting to be filled.

Why hadn't she been a bit like this Madam character? Taking the initiative for once? Damn it, why were women such opposites? Either sexually starved vampires, clawing at a man for his rod, or sexually retarded, like Esther. Why couldn't they just have understandable needs, like men? Like him?

He pulled against his bonds. The stretched position was beginning to make his muscles complain. Even as he thought it, his calf muscles spasmed. He cried out in agony, unable to move to relieve the awful contraction.

Suddenly the door opened again. She was there. 'What's the matter?' She sounded genuinely concerned.

'Cramp,' he gasped.

'Ah, I didn't think of that. Where?' He told her, and she began to knead his cramping muscles with firm fingers. 'I guess you could do with some exercise.'

'Yes,' he agreed instantly, seeing the chance of escape. 'Exercise, that's the answer.'

A cold flannel wrapped around his mouth and nose. He inhaled a strange smell, felt his senses swim and tried to pull his face away, but her hand followed his nose, and consciousness receded.

When he came too, something had changed. He realised that he was no longer spread-eagled. Had it all been a horrible dream? He wriggled experimentally. His hands were by his sides, but they were not free. Nothing was free. His hands were glued to his thighs, his elbows to his sides, and his knees and ankles were bonded together.

'What the?' he said, his speech strangely slurred.

'I thought you might like a change of scenery.'

It was her. He was still there, wherever there was, at the mercy of his unknown tormentor. Only now he was wrapped, something like a caterpillar, in a web of straps. He was still lying on the bed, but could do no more than flex his joined knees. His hands, rather disconcertingly, seemed to be in pockets of leather, and no amount of wrenching and pulling would free them. She pulled his feet over the side, heaved his shoulders. He sat up on the edge of the bed.

'What now?' he said irritably, his senses slowly returning. He could feel straps around his neck, chest, middle, upper thigh, above and below the knee, and ankle, and as he strained, he became aware that they were all joined together from top to bottom.

'First we eat,' she said. 'Then we have some more fun.'

Kevin didn't like the sound of that.

'Open wide,' she urged.

'What for?' he said defensively.

'One last chance. Eat or don't, I don't care.'

He opened his mouth, and was spoon-fed some pap like a baby.

'That's all,' she said after a few mouthfuls.

'But I'm still hungry,' he complained.

'You might have some cravings, but that was adequate. Any more and you'll get fat. And we can't have that, now can we?'

'It's my body. If I want to get fat, I'll bloody-well do so.'

She chuckled. 'Not here, you won't.'

His head cocked worriedly inside the blindfold, and he felt something tighten and begin to lift him up and forwards. 'Aaaah!' he yelled, expecting to fall flat n his face, unable to lift his hands to his aid. But instead his knees buckled just slightly, and the slack was taken up. He bounced. He pulled with anger against this new indignity, and just bounced some more. He was strung up on something elastic, just like a baby-bouncer, he realised. He wailed his displeasure.

'Right,' said the female. 'Now you can get all the exercise you need. Work some of that flab off.'

'I will not!' he howled indignantly. 'Let me out of this thing!'

'The fun is just starting,' she said. 'Ready? Now, bend your knees, and jump.'

He gritted his teeth and stayed still. There was a faint whistle, and he screeched with shock as something cut around his thighs. His legs flexed and he bounced away from the pain. 'Ow! You hit me, you bitch!'

'Now bounce!'

'I will not... eeaagh!'

Suddenly he stopped bouncing. He had been wound up so that his feet were off the floor, and he realised there must be something attaching his ankles to the floor, for his powers of movement were suddenly totally constricted. 'What now?' he said angrily, twisting and tugging against the bonds.

'You're making much too much noise,' she said,

efficiently popping a bar between his teeth as he opened his mouth to complain. 'It's affecting my concentration. I will enjoy this so much more if you shut up.'

Kevin's eyes nearly popped out with anger as the straps of the gag were tightened under his chin and around his head. It didn't actually stop the noise, but it certainly stopped his words from being comprehensible. Even though, from the vitriolic garble, one could probably guess the content.

Then he was lowered back onto his feet.

His first hint of what was to come was a faint whistle followed by a loud smack as the thin leather hit his bare legs. Kevin squealed, danced, bounced and gyrated on the end of the rubber spring as the unknown female plastered his bound body with weals. He screamed wordless abuse as his body flexed and bounded away from the sting of the lash. But he could neither see where they were coming from nor avoid the strokes. He thought for a few moments that he must be in hell. Never had he experienced such total helplessness.

When she stopped he was panting hard. It took him a moment to register the fact, and he stood there, still tautly waiting for further punishment, wondering if this cessation was some ruse. His leather cage was wound up taut. He froze on tiptoe. What was she going to do next?

Then she began to writhe around his body in a sexual frenzy. He felt bare breasts against his buttocks as she knelt behind him, and her hands began to tease and play with his cock. His skin, sensitive from the lashing, crawled beneath her fingers. He groaned with the combined rasping pain and eroticism of her now-gentle touch.

Unable to escape, he stood there while her hands wreaked deadly work upon his cock and her tongue licked up his sore back, evoking conflicting signals of pain and longing. He moaned through the gag, but as his cock began to lurch into rigidity, and his tightly bound legs constricted his tightening balls, his whole body became a mass of eroticism, every inch of flesh sensitised and eager for the touch of this woman. Not any woman, but this woman. This siren. This witch.

She twisted his cocooned body around, and he moaned and thrust himself at her, but she did not relieve the ache between his legs. Her fingers and tongue carried on smoothing away at all parts of him. Then she was behind him again, her arms wrapped around his bound ones, and she was twirling his nipples between finger and thumb. Blood pulsed into his cock until he thought it would explode. Then she was touching him there again... and something was passed around the base of his erection and tightened. The constriction was painfully, making him groan with unexpected pleasure.

A finger then slid between his clamped buttocks and began to rub against his anus. Jolts of pleasure were firing from the core of his being into every nerve in his body. It couldn't get any more tense, any more beautifully sexual, he thought.

Her finger began to penetrate him.

He gasped and writhed in the exquisite pleasure of that invasion as her finger went in and out, greasing, enlarging, softening his clenched muscle. Then something pushed against him, which was not her finger. A cry was wrenched from between his bound jaws as he stretched and stretched to accommodate something alien in that most private of places. Dear God, what was she doing to him?

A deft turn of her wrist and vibrations began to permeate his body from within; alien, strange, and wonderful pulses that reached out towards his sexual organs. His muscles spasmed with shocked delight.

He was moaning deep in his throat, hanging helplessly in the spider's cocoon, and once more she stepped back and began to whip him. His mind descended deep into the sexual core of his being. Now every lash of the whip, every flinch of his body was an erotic torment doubled by the constrictions which bound his nether regions. He moaned, but not in dismay, for he had no idea that he had moaned. His libido engulfed his awareness until a chance flick of the whip kissed the tip of his penis. With the force of an explosion he erupted on to the floor.

There was silence.

And in that silence he gradually awoke to an awareness of what he had just been through, and the awful comprehension that he had been force-fed with the most wonderful, mind-bending experience he had ever had in his life. He had been injected with a mind-dependency drug and he knew he wanted it again and again and again and again.

Within his mask and behind his gag he wept for Esther. He had never before known the exquisite sexuality of pain, and knew she could never satisfy him again with her trusting dependence.

When the dominatrix came in later and lay him back upon the bed he was almost compliant, having attained a desperate acceptance of her domination over him.

Back upstairs, Esther hummed happily as she ironed. A strange warmth kept invading her tummy and muscling its way between her legs. She felt herself moisten there. Very carefully she unplugged the iron, folded up the board and put it away, and made her way to their empty bedroom. She danced a small dance as she threw off her clothes, swirling them around her head and throwing them in abandonment all over the bedroom. She looked in the mirror, made a moue of her lips and pushed her breasts together with her hands, then she threw herself down onto the bed and closed her eyes. Kevin tied up, at her mercy. Pleasurable spasms flashed through her aroused body. Kevin alone in a soundproofed garage. She listened. Could she hear anything? No.

She lay back and opened her legs and began to rub a forefinger gently up and down between them. She was already slick with need. Her smile stretched into a gasp. Her legs flailed over the bed. Blood pulsed through her breasts. Her finger moved faster and faster. Her breath began to shorten. Then it became a gasp. It was coming! Ah! A single, fleeting, blindingly beautiful moment when something exploded deep inside her sex, ran like electricity to her fingertips and toes. A slow pulse, a rippling outwards. She counted with held breath, stilled finger pressing on the spot...

She lay for a moment revelling in the spread of warmth that lingered from the orgasm, and her breathing began to slow. She thought of Kevin, lying alone in darkness, unable to touch himself. A slow smile dawned. A feline smile. She yawned, stretched, spread her limbs over his side of the bed, and dropped instantly into a sound sleep.

In the morning she showered, dressed, and went out.

'Hello darlin', where's hubby today?' the chap at the petrol station asked, taking her credit card. The hubby usually filled the car without fail at seven on a Monday, and it was now Wednesday.

She assessed him with new eyes. He was not too bright, but was attractive in a sexual kind of way, and for some reason his familiarity did not offend her as it had in the past. Instead, she returned his open appraisal with one of her own. It was kind of fun looking at people, and imagining them strapped up in Madam's room. She could take that superior expression off his face in a single stroke. The thought made her smile.

'Kevin's a bit indisposed today,' she said, insinuating all sorts of suggestions into the soft words. 'But I'm going to look after him, and make him better.'

The garage attendant's eyes widened as he clearly thought he'd like to have her making him better. Esther smiled inwardly at his response. Oh yes, she was going to make him much, much better. She drove on into town to do some shopping without Kevin's overshadowing presence dictating what she bought. She got herself a new pair of jeans. Tight ones. She kept them on, wearing them around the town with enjoyment, wiggling her hips. Someone wolf-whistled, and though she knew better than to turn round and search the crowd for that quick grin which would have given him away, she knew it was for her, and it felt good.

Then she went and had her hair cut in a ragged, fuzzy blonde halo.

She bought herself a little red lacy top – cheap and flirty

– and a pair of heeled shoes in the same colour.

Then she sat at a table outside a cafe, bought herself a cup of coffee and a big sticky bun, and ogled the men who were ogling her.

Chapter Six

'Kevin?' Esther shook him. 'Kevin, wake up. You'll be late for work.'

Kevin sat up in sudden shock. It took a moment to register the fact that he was in his own room, in his own bed, and Esther was staring at him, concern in her eyes. 'What have you done to your lovely hair?' he demanded, dazed, not knowing what else to say.

Esther hid her amusement behind brows raised with apparent sarcasm. 'You don't recall? I'm not surprised, but last night it came out as more of a compliment. You told me it looked really sexy.'

'I said that?' He had always liked her long hair, it was very feminine, he thought. She looked older, somehow, with her hair short. Less – what was it? – that was it! Less naïve. But as she carried on his heartbeat increased in panic.

'That wasn't all you said. I thought you'd had a bit too much to drink when you came home in a taxi, but I was still a bit surprised that the poor man had to help you up to the front door. You were babbling nonsense, Kevin. I was most embarrassed, it's not like you at all.'

'What was I saying?' Kevin asked warily.

'I couldn't make it out. Something about bonds – equity bonds, I think – oh, yes, and something about whipping someone into shape. Perhaps you should stay home today, you really don't seem at all like yourself.'

'Today? What day is today?'

'Wednesday, of course.'

'Wednesday?' Had he only been away three nights? It seemed like a week. He was utterly confused. So, he had come back by taxi last night, he thought he vaguely recalled as much, but why had the cow let him go? He pressed fingers to his temples and Esther became instantly contrite, her voice soothing, her hand testing his forehead for temperature.

'Oh, poor Kevin, I'm being a real nag. You're not feeling very well at all, are you? Perhaps you've got a dose of food poisoning from something you ate at the hotel. You really don't seem like your usual self. I do think you should stay at home today. Let me call you in sick, tell them that they're pushing you too hard. It's not acceptable, the amount of meetings you have to go to these days.'

'Oh, no,' he said frantically. 'I'd better go in. Must have a lot of work to catch up on. I'll be all right. I could do with a cup of tea, though, honey.'

After she had gone downstairs he looked at his wrists, his arms, his legs, but there was not the hint of a mark to be seen. He scratched his hands through his hair, stretched, and yawned. Had he been dreaming? But in spite of the fact that he had no marks, he ached in places he shouldn't be aching. Someone really had had him trussed up in a soundproofed room. But if that was so, what had happened to her assertion that she would keep him forever? Had she had a change of heart? Somehow that didn't fit with the character.

He scrabbled out of bed and stood for a while under the

shower letting the hot water run over his body, and gradually his experience began to become less real. After a while he gave a doubtful laugh; Christ, what an experience. It hadn't been all bad, at that. Shame he didn't dare tell anyone about it.

Esther smiled to herself as she saw her husband off for the day. He would be so confused, and would probably simply feign illness because he had no rational explanation of his absence. When she guessed he would also feel guilty and do his utmost to prevent her from phoning in to work with her irritation, she was right. On arrival home that evening he came armed with a bunch of flowers.

He was also comfortingly attentive, as though trying to prove to himself that he had done his wife no injustice, and for the first time she saw behind the façade. It made her think back on all the other times he had come home with boxes of chocolates or flowers. The expression 'guilt payments' came strongly to mind. Goodness, how many women had he been with, the bastard? She also wondered how long this present bout of loyalty would last.

That over with, as far as Kevin was concerned, everything was back to normal, and that night he informed Esther, 'We have to attend one of those company socials on Saturday evening. The chairman only told me today. Apparently we're trying to sweet-talk a new bank into going along with our latest project in the city. He's asked for you to be there. I'm really sorry, I know you find these functions a bit of a bore, but it's important to my career.'

Esther had been looking forward to the weekend herself. She'd had her own plans all worked out. Though he didn't realise it, they included Kevin. Her disappointment showed. 'Must we?'

He kissed her briefly on the cheek. 'The chairman is pushing this family firm thing until it's getting up my nose. I'm afraid I really need you to be there. Do it for me, honey? Pretty please? I'll take you out and buy you a new dress. We can show our faces and leave early, if you like.'

'Please don't call me honey.'

Reading between the lines, she realised Kevin didn't want her there at all, but if the chairman was going to insist, what could he do? Poor Kevin. Having to take his little dab of a wife out must make him feel quite inferior. It would also cramp his style; she would have to do something about that. Perhaps it was time, after all. She was about to agree, but Kevin was still talking.

'Don't worry if you don't understand what they're going on about. Just agree with everything anyone says, Essie, and we'll get along fine.'

She smiled sweetly at him, seething at his condescending manner. How long had he talked to her like that? She couldn't recall. 'I think I can manage that, dear. But I think I'll go into town and buy myself a new dress while you're at work. I realised last time that what I was wearing wasn't quite appropriate. In fact, I might buy two or three if your firm is going to make a habit of this. I really don't want to be the one to stand in the way of your promotion. I know how much it means to you.'

He looked instantly worried. He knew how much dresses cost. 'Wait until Saturday morning, and I'll drive you in and help you choose.'

She replied pensively, kissing him on the cheek. 'No, I

think that will be too late. If I don't find something I like I won't have time to shop around. Besides, this will be my little surprise for you. I know you well enough by now to know your tastes in women's clothes. I won't let you down, I promise.'

He gave in and smiled tolerantly. 'Well, if you're sure you want to go on your own, sugar. Just don't let anyone rip you off with designer labels.'

'I wouldn't dream of it,' she replied.

It was just as well he didn't see her go into town, for he would hardly have recognised the self-confident woman who marched from shop to shop. She knew exactly what she wanted all right, and it took a while to find it. But this time she had no husband to take her round by the arm and talk to the shop assistants on her behalf, as if she was incapable of doing it for herself.

'Can I help, madam?' The thin assistant looked over her glasses at Esther's present attire, her narrow eyes seemingly calculating to a penny what type of dress the client could afford, and assessing it wasn't going to be one from her shop.

'Madam would like to try on that black dress in the window,' she responded, with sarcasm.

The shop assistant's manner gradually altered, and what with the sale of two rather expensive little numbers and a pile of silky underwear, she made a reasonable bit of commission, all things considered.

Esther then went on to a jewellery shop to purchase some costume jewellery that was almost obscenely ostentatious. Luckily it was not as expensive as it looked, though she doubted Kevin would know the difference. She enjoyed shopping for herself, and realised how often she had simply shopped with Kevin in mind. How easily she had forgotten to be herself. She was beginning to look forward to Saturday night with the gleeful anticipation of a teenager.

Saturday evening she dressed quickly, and shrouded herself in the ankle-length, plain black evening cape she had always hated because she felt silly in it. She now realised what it was for.

'Essie, honey, that looks lovely,' Kevin said, gratification on his face. The cape had been a Christmas present from him, and she had never seemed even slightly interested in it. He thought it chic. Esther thought it covered a lot. She was glad he didn't look down, though, because it didn't cover her shoes, which were tiny and strappy and high-heeled: a dead give-away.

When they arrived at the hotel she kissed him on the cheek. 'Go on in and get me a gin, darling. I just have to go and powder my nose.'

'You don't want me to wait?' He was confused at her self-sufficiency. She normally hated walking into a room full of unknown people without an escort.

She gave him a gentle shove in the back, clutching her make-up bag beneath the cape. 'Go on in. I'm not sixteen. I can cope.'

'Well, if you're sure...'

The function room was large. Kevin liked it because it had a sort of old-English charm, he said. Esther knew the truth; the hotel was posh and expensive and he hoped to patronise it on his own salary one day.

As he entered he fixed a professional smile in place, and greeted his work colleagues and the dark-suited bankers with his almost upper crust disdain. Very soon he stood with a drink in his hand, engaged in serious conversation with a tall greying man with the eyes of a crocodile.

Suddenly the man's protuberant eyes popped even further. 'Oh my,' he said, dwelling heavily on each word. 'Oh my, oh my! Who is that woman?'

Kevin looked around, choked on his drink, spluttered and coughed. 'That's my wife!' he gasped in horror.

Esther was dressed in the shortest black cocktail dress he had ever seen, and wore extremely high heels, all of which accentuated the shapely outline of her long legs. Not only that, her newly shorn hair was sort of frizzed up, her face was exquisitely made-up, and her earrings nearly reached the expanse of unblemished white flesh of her shoulders.

She gave him a warm smile from across the room, and her hips seemed to gyrate as she walked towards him. 'Jesus,' he muttered, stunned to petrifaction.

The banker turned to him. 'She can still make you feel like that and you're married to her?'

Kevin stared at him, then back to his wife, then around at the other men. He saw lust in their eyes and they all pulled in their paunches slightly as she approached.

'Do you like my new dress, darling?' she asked huskily, draping herself around him.

'I – I expected there to be a bit more of it,' he managed to blurt.

The banker roared with laughter and clapped him on the shoulder. 'I like you, fellow,' he said. 'You and your charming wife must sit with me.'

Kevin gave a little helpless shrug, suddenly feeling out of his depth. What the hell had happened to Esther? She was going to embarrass the hell out of him. What was she playing at?

But she didn't embarrass him. The banker, he soon realised, was an accomplished lecher, and Esther seemed to take it all in her stride. From the other side of the table he couldn't quite see but he was sure the man's hand dwelt under the table more often and for longer than was strictly necessary. And the banker's wife, whom he felt obliged to engage in conversation, was a dry and humourless woman who bored him silly by just agreeing with everything he said. To his further annoyance, across the table, Esther seemed to be encouraging the man, giggling at his jokes and sexual sallies.

When they began to mix after the dinner – softening the target, his boss called it – Esther hung faithfully to Kevin's arm. This not only kept him continually surrounded by a pack of drooling admirers intent on buying her next drink, but it also put him flush to the most prestigious of his guests, something he would normally have been ecstatic about. He knew this would be followed the next day by a taxing debriefing session – how much information had he wheedle out of his mark – but for the first time in his life, Kevin didn't wheedle much. He spent the evening in shock, and far from feeling like continually apologising patronisingly for his unworldly little wife, he found himself in the strange position of being jealous of all those men who craved introduction to her. Before the evening was out he found himself invited to a dinner evening with the Mansells, company directors who had always ignored him before. He knew it was her fault. Fault? He had been angling for such an honour for longer than he would admit, and she had achieved it. What he wasn't quite sure, was how or why, and most of all he didn't understand the anger that filled him at the thought of his wife behaving like a tart all evening. Even though he had to admit to himself, she was stunning. If he had not been married to her, she was the kind he sure as hell would have made a pass at.

As they drove home he kept giving her sidelong glances. 'Are you out of your mind?' he said finally. 'You could have made me the laughing stock of the bank.'

'I rather got the impression the men weren't laughing.'

'No,' he said darkly, holding her elbow possessively as she hobbled up to the front door on feet that obviously hurt. All night his cock had been doing somersaults, almost as if she were someone else's wife and he the lecher. And on the heels of his lust was the greatest feeling of jealousy he had ever experienced. It all added up to one great itch which needed servicing. And she was asking for it, he found himself thinking. Before he was quite aware of his own intentions, he had kicked the door shut behind them and slammed her up against the wall in the hall.

He couldn't get his trousers undone quick enough, and while he was still fumbling he was sucking mouthfuls of succulent breast which he thumbed easily from her indecent neckline. When he was free he rubbed shaky hands up under her dress, over the smooth expanse of her tights, and ripped. Then, wedging her up against the easy-clean wallpaper he lifted her onto his spearing erection with a great groan.

Esther gasped as she sank onto him. His sudden and unexpected attack sent massive shock waves through her. She closed her eyes and indulged in her secret fantasy. She was a housewife. This big, strong, beautiful man had just burst his way in through the door, ripped her clothes off, and was raping her in her own hall because she was so desirable he could not help himself. She groaned out loud.

'Fuck,' Kevin cursed, hearing this new sound. 'I've hurt you.'

'No, no,' she said urgently, sucking at his ear, and her voice was low and husky with the euphoria of sex. 'Don't stop. Ram me. Hard.'

He rammed. Having been rampant half the evening there was no way he could be gentle or hold back. It was all or nothing, and he was past stopping. All too soon he came, a painful explosion he could not have stopped had he wanted to.

Quickly he plummeted down to earth. 'Darling, I...'

She put a finger to his lips. 'Don't apologise.'

'But I...'

'I enjoyed it.'

He was taken aback. 'You did?'

She kissed his nose. 'I enjoyed the whole evening. It was fun. Thank you. Come and have a night-cap with me before we turn in.'

They sat in silent, contemplative companionship for a short while, and drank to the success of the evening. Then

Esther went up to bed first, as she always did, while Kevin sat in confused solitude for a moment. The bankers had certainly gone away sounding positive about the deal, and he was not unaware of the part his wife had unwittingly played. High finance and sex, it seemed, were interwoven, and if one was good, so was the other. He hadn't felt that strongly stirred by Esther for an awfully long time. He vaguely recalled that sex had been more exiting when they were courting, and that after they married things got sort of routine. He had supposed that was just what happened.

This new sexual excitement stirred his loins and before he realised it was happening, his tired prick was valiantly rising again, leaving him feeling more confused than ever; even when courting, once an evening had been enough. He thought back. Esther hadn't been a virgin when he'd met her, but she had been acquiescent and accepting. Her subservient role had made him feel confident and protective, and therefore dominant. For a long time now sex had been a mutual and unspoken agreement, a hasty fumble of removed clothing in the dark, and a fairly rapid consummation after which they both fell asleep.

That was why it was so different with the other women. The secretaries, colleagues' wives. It wasn't the consummation that excited him so much as the chase. The sex, in the end, was much the same with any female and, no matter how much the women made come-hither eyes at him, he never went back to the same woman twice – apart from his wife. That was his particular brand of loyalty. For in his way, he was truly loyal. He had promised to love and cherish, and he did so. He'd often thought it wasn't fair that men had appetites a wife was incapable of fulfilling. Yet that dominatrix woman had an appetite the like of which he had never seen.

He gave a short laugh at his own musings; obviously because he wished it could be that way, that was all. He told himself to stop daydreaming and get back to reality.

He had believed for a long time that the elusive and explosive sexual experience of which couples often boasted was obviously a fabrication. The sort of women who made sensible wives had been designed to be the recipients for a man's seed, and that was all. After that they fulfilled their own emotional needs with the messy and annoying process of child-rearing, leaving the male partner space to get on with his time-consuming process of hunting for further conquests.

Yet the woman who kidnapped him had enjoyed an orgasm. And suddenly, out of the blue, so had Esther. Even during the exquisite experience with her in the hall, when he let himself down and turned into the original caveman, he had felt her orgasm. What was going on?

Confused, he crept into bed quietly next to his sleeping wife, bringing with him a newly-awakened need for her which wouldn't seem to go away. He wished Esther could now and again be like that other woman, tie him up and make him feel exquisitely helpless, then play with his prick, bring him to fruition with her hand. He felt guilty, as though this desire were a betrayal of his marriage vows, but he could not help himself. And as he lay there, his hips moving just slightly in recollection, he realised with irritation that he had a real snorter of a hard-on that wasn't simply going to go away because he was tired.

Esther moved, turned over.

He froze.

When, to his shock, he felt a hand slowly slide to his groin, it was hard to keep back the groan that crept to his lips. But it was only when her teeth gently began to nibble his arm did he realise she was awake and knew exactly what she was doing. Shock kept him rigid. Esther never instigated sex. Well, only inasmuch as she would go up to bed, coyly letting him know she would be waiting. But her hand was undeniably beginning to caress him, tightening his balls and sending juices dribbling onto his belly.

He lay tense, staring into the darkness, not knowing how to react. Esther's caresses became more urgent, her nipping teeth more painful, and then her body was writhing against his. His breath began to shorten, need becoming a driving force that stole every ounce of willpower he had left. Somehow she had moved so his hand lay between her legs, and as she moved his fingers began to toy with the wetness he unexpectedly discovered there. She groaned, and this time he heard it as a low sound of animal need.

He began to move, but abruptly Esther's hand pressed his shoulder back to the bed, and she slid herself on top of him. Esther on top? He stared up, seeing just the outline of her above him, the bulbous mass of her breasts, the frizz of her short hair. For a second he had a sense of *déjà vu*; he had seen this alluring image before – but where?

Then she bent down, brushed his lips with hers, and began to kiss him.

Quite when his shock turned to pure lust he was not sure, but within moments his rampant cock was up inside her, and she was riding him with an enthusiasm which made him forget who she was and where he was. It could have been anyone, anywhere – he just needed to come so badly it hurt. He grabbed her shoulders and used his strength to move her more quickly up and down his shaft until it became a vibrant volcano that suddenly erupted. She sat still on him while his spasms died, until his breath returned, and he knew she was staring down at him in the darkness. He opened his mouth to speak, but she put a fingertip to his lips.

'Don't spoil it,' she whispered. 'Don't apologise.'

Chapter Seven

Kevin walked in a different kind of euphoria for a few days, and couldn't really understand it himself. After the business evening he had shocked himself not only by taking Esther in the hallway, but by the sheer ferocity of that coupling. To his mind he had betrayed a side of him that it was better she did not know. What on earth had he been thinking of?

Yet what had happened later had been even more incomprehensible. Esther must have had a mild breakdown, or something, because of his actions. He knew one thing with certainty: it mustn't happen again. He realised the only way to rid himself of this awful compulsion for sex was to go out and get another girl as soon as possible. The more he thought about it, the more acceptable an answer it seemed to be. If he didn't get his quota of sexual fixes he knew he would go mad or attack Esther again, and he was terribly afraid that if he did so, he might shock her to the extent she would leave him. Despite his infidelities, he didn't want that.

When the new temp, Louise, had first begun to make interested eyes towards him he had been a bit standoffish, revelling in the renewal of marital bliss. But things had changed. She was not his usual type; dressed like a punk in black torn clothes, with her bright orange hair and overpowering make-up, but she did have a bubbly and outgoing nature. And she had quite a set of knockers, too.

After a little bit of judicious questioning, he discovered his firm had only employed her because the agency had not been entirely honest about her appearance. Not that he found it unattractive; in its own way the overtly unfeminine garb was quite a turn-on, even though it was not what his preconceived ideas of women were all about. Yet the more he looked at her, and the more she gave back that sly little grin of awareness, the more attractive she seemed to become. He found her open lack of respect for gender convention faintly off-putting yet, at the same time, strangely compelling. She was available, she clearly found him attractive and was making no effort to hide her feelings, and it didn't take him long to wonder what kind of person she was under all that make-up, and whether she was really as open about sex as he thought she might be.

Once he began to imagine her without clothes on, it took even less time for him to make the mental jump to actually figuring out how he was going to work it. With a confident smile he realised he was back on track. He preened inwardly; Kevin the stud was going to break another ride.

It took a couple of days of insinuations and a couple more of adventurous groping before Kevin finally took the plunge. Accidentally bumping into her on the way out to the car park, he put on his best charming smile. 'I can't help noticing you're a really attractive young lady, Louise,' he gushed.

She gave him a sidelong glance. 'I know what you've been noticing, mate, and there are two of 'em. But you're not bad yourself, for a smart-arse banker. Got a nice tight bum, too. I like that in a man.'

He was slightly taken aback, but passed it off with a chuckle and a sly comment. 'Do you always check out men's bums?'

'Same way as you check out women's tits, banker.'

'My name is Kevin.'

She grinned. 'Okay, Kev. Your place or mine?'

'Pardon?'

'Come off it. You want a bit of fun, I want a bit of fun, so how about now?'

He was almost disconcerted at the abruptness of her; he wasn't used to that at all. For a moment they carried on walking, then Louise stopped by a 2CV that had been painted by hand, bringing Kevin back to earth with a thud. What was he doing? If she was always this casual, how many other men and clambered inside her knickers? It didn't seem that much clambering was required. Hell, they would probably fall off if he crooked his little finger. His prick, however, knew no such hesitation, and he found himself speaking again. 'How about Saturday?'

'Sounds fine by me.'

'I know a nice little hotel...'

'My place is better.' She gave a broad smile, and winked. 'Plenty of room for innovation, and we won't be disturbed by room service.'

'So where do you live?'

'Meet me at the supermarket car park over there, lunchtime on Saturday, and I'll drive. That way no one will see your car at my place. I know you're married.'

'Don't you mind that?'

'Hell, no. Older men are usually less prudish than the young studs, and married is safer. I'm not stupid enough to get myself tied to some lovesick teenager when I'm just nineteen.'

Older men? Kevin was slightly hurt by the assumption that she considered him old, and slightly shocked to find she was only nineteen, but as his eyes greedily devoured her generous bosom, he found himself becoming even more excited by the prospect than he had been before. If Esther hadn't been waiting for him he would have quite happily followed her home right away. 'Two days' time, then,' he said, with a certain amount of gung-ho bravado.

'Okay stud. I'll see what you're made of on Saturday. TTFN, stud.'

He strutted back to his car as she zoomed off. Bloody hell – nineteen and fancying him. In that moment everything he had learned over the past few weeks went straight out of the window. He would give the little whore a rogering on Saturday she would remember for a long while.

By Saturday Kevin's excitement had been dulled only slightly by the fact that he had lied to Esther about a weekend meeting in the city for the first time in ages. She had smiled happily and waved him off, but there had been a kind of sadness in her gaze, almost as if she knew what he was doing. But how the hell could she know? One thing he prided himself on was his discretion. He had never once let Esther know he had not been faithful to her. He really didn't want to hurt her.

And there he was, sitting in his car in the supermarket,

feeling slightly miserable, wondering if Louise was indeed going to turn up, or whether she'd got cold feet. He would feel pretty silly booking himself into a hotel for a lonely night if she didn't come, because he wouldn't dare go home till Sunday.

Then a horn blared behind him. Still dressed in black, but this time with fluorescent green hair, she was grinning like a Cheshire cat as she leaned over to unlock the passenger door. 'Hi there, get in,' she beamed.

He pressed the remote that worked the central locking system on his company car, and squeezed himself into the bucket seat by her side. The whole car smelled of something sweet and probably illegal, and he wondered, once again, what the hell he was doing.

But Louise clearly knew no such misgivings; she slammed the car into gear and screeched away with an acceleration that surprised him. 'This is going to be fun,' she said. 'I've been looking forward to this. I know your type. You like to dominate, don't you? I can see it in your eyes. I brought these in case you wanted to use them.' She indicated a pair of handcuffs that were sitting openly on the dashboard.

Kevin blushed slightly, grabbed them, and put them on his lap, out of sight of other drivers. Louise had her eyes on the road, and didn't seem to notice his awkwardness.

'I've got just about everything in the pad. Restraints, gags, beaters, you name it. The place has got a fantastic beam, too. Ideal for bondage.' She elbowed him in the ribs. 'Nearly there, just round the corner.'

'The pad' didn't look like a residential building, and Kevin found himself swivelling in the seat with apprehension. It looked more like a dockside warehouse than a place someone lived. However, there were a few more cars in a small car park, and when they entered the foyer he realised the warehouse had been turned into flats. Huge flats. The blossoming realisation that Louise's accent and choice of clothes and car were not indicative of her financial status was proven as she opened a rather functional door into a vast room, which was ablaze with sunshine. Great banks of windows down one side looked out over a river area which had once been docks and was in the process of being turned into a leisure complex, and the inside of the room was obviously and outrageously designer-born.

'Daddy bought it for me,' she said, throwing her woven ethnic bag onto a leather sofa, and joining him at the window. 'Great, isn't it?'

Kevin swallowed his irritation. Why should she have all this just because daddy bought it for her, the little cow?

Louise pressed a button and blinds began to roll down electrically over the windows, shutting out the daylight. She pressed another switch, and red light filtered down from the high ceiling. She wandered over and lit a couple of josticks, and the room instantly became a whore's boudoir.

'Blimey,' Kevin said, impressed despite his jealousy. Louise grinned at his awe, and pressed another switch. There was the small whine of a motor and a hook descended from one of the beams. He was under no illusions as to its intended use. 'Now let's get this straight,' aid. 'I'm the one who's going to be dominant, here?

She bent over, pulling a box from under her bed. 'There are wooden structures by the stairs which can be useful, especially that half-banister. There's the bed, there's the beam, and there are various attachments on this wall. The rest of the stuff is in that chest. Would you like a drink before we start?'

'Yes, please,' he said fervently, not feeling at all sexy. It was too organised, somehow, and turned him right off.

She opened a cabinet which was filled with every kind of drink under the sun. 'Gin?'

'Whisky – on the rocks,' he said. 'Why in hell do you temp when you've got all this?' he asked.

'Because I enjoy it. Christ, I'd get bored sitting at home all day. Anybody would. God knows how women can do that. Must turn them into mushrooms.' She knocked back her gin as if it was water.

Kevin thought guiltily about Esther. There had been a couple of times she'd indicated she'd like a job, and he had laughed at the idea of his wife needing to work. Did she feel like that? He liked his wife to be not working; it made him feel much more like the provider, the man of the house, but it hadn't really occurred to him that a woman could be bored with being a housewife. It was what they were supposed to be, wasn't it? And he'd often said he'd give his eye-teeth for the chance to sit at home and do nothing. For the first time, he wondered if that was true.

The whisky began to warm his insides. He wasn't used to drinking spirits in the middle of the day. Come to think of it, he wasn't used to having steamy sex in the middle of the day, let alone bondage sessions.

Louise was standing there with her hands on her hips,

her head to one side. 'Are you getting cold feet, buster? Aren't your balls big enough for this? Are you only capable of bonking silly bimbos in hotel rooms?'

'Christ, you're a mouthy little thing, aren't you?' Kevin snapped, irritated.

'I've heard the rumours. That was why I thought you had more spunk.' Her foot began to tap on the floor, then she turned and flounced to the door. 'If you don't want to do it, fine. Just walk on out of here, and maybe just after you're gone I'll give your sweet little wife a call to say how you can't get it up any more. Who knows, perhaps honey-bunch will be pleased.'

'My number's unlisted,' he sneered smugly, not believing she'd carry out the threat, even if she did have his home number.

She grinned, picked up a mobile phone from her bag, and tapped in a number. Kevin stood there watching, a sense of unreality creeping over him. Even from where he was he could hear the ringing tone. Then there was the sound of a voice, tiny, but recognisable. 'Hello... Hello? Who is this?'

He took an angry step towards Louise, wrenched the phone from her hand, and thrust her backward onto the bed as he cancelled the call. Throwing the telephone aside he put a knee on her chest and pinned her wrists back up above her head. 'You bitch,' he said, then stopped. They stared at each other, face to face for a moment, and Kevin could see she was flushed and panting. 'This is what you wanted all along, isn't it?' he panted.

She said nothing, but pulled fractionally at the confinement of his hands around her wrists as though testing his strength. He tightened his hold. She wriggled slightly harder, then lifted a leg and kneed him in the ribs. It hurt, but he retained his grip, shifting his body so she couldn't do that a second time. 'Oh, we like to play rough, do we? Well, two can play at that game, darling.'

He flipped her over onto her front and put a knee in the small of her back, the power and weight differential evident in the ease with which he held her there while he leaned back and dragged a rope from the chest. Despite her furious struggles he bound her hands behind her back, then crossed her ankles and dragged them up behind her, hog-tying her with one end of the rope so that her knees splayed out. Then he lifted her head by her tangled green hair and wrapped the other end of the rope around her mouth so she was arched back by the makeshift gag.

To his surprise he found himself buzzing with the excitement of tying her up, and was warming to the event quite nicely. 'I saw that one in a magazine,' he said conversationally. 'I think you'll find you can't get out of it.'

She struggled against the bonds, making grunting noises, but Kevin realised she was not upset at all, just really turned on by her lack of control. He also realised quite suddenly that this was for real. This was what the bitch wanted. She wanted to be used and abused; it was what she thrived on. He sat on the bed beside her and inserted a hand into her garments, searching and finding a nipple to toy with. She groaned and squirmed at his touch, and his own arousal was galvanised into action. Swivelling her around on the bed, he put his hands into her skirt and yanked her knickers down, forcing them over her knees until they dangled on her crossed ankles. She was panting with anticipation as he smoothed both hands up over her tight buttocks.

His prick throbbed, the tightness of his trousers an almost painful constriction as his erection pumped into being. He felt his breath shortening with anticipation as he thrust a finger between her thighs to find she was already wet and slick and ready. From his experience at the hands of the not-so-lovely Michelle a couple of months back, he knew that she was aroused simply by the action of being tied up, something he would not have really believed had it not happened to himself.

Trembling slightly he slipped down to kneel at the side of the low bed, unzipped his trousers and thrust them down over his thighs. He pulled Louise towards him and tempted his rampant erection with the sight of the exposed female sex as he untied her ankles. Now he was able to pull her off the edge of the bed to slip her vagina cosily onto his ready cock. She knelt before him in an arc, her neck still bent back towards him by the rope gag attached to her wrists, her breasts jutting out wantonly into his seeking hands. He ripped the fabric from them, not caring about the damage he was doing to her clothes, and grasped handfuls of her generous bosom as he began to move in and out of her in long leisurely strokes, sighing with the sheer eroticism of having this tight and nubile body at his disposal, to use as he pleased. Oh God, he thought, it was beautiful.

She moaned a little, her hands working behind her, but was not interested in whether she was comfortable or not. All he was interested in was pleasing himself, and it was good. Slowly he rubbed himself to explosive heights inside her, his prick enjoying every gliding, sensitising movement, while his hands worked at her breasts, kneading, pinching her large nipples into erection with finger and thumb as he pleasured himself, thrusting for deeper penetration. Then the novelty of the occasion became too much. He felt an incredible buzzing in his loins and thrust his hips violently a few times until he came, pulsing deep inside her.

When he was done the euphoria diminished to a faintly comfortable aftermath. He pulled away and released the rope from her mouth, leaving her hands tied securely.

'That good, bitch?' he mocked.

'Hell,' she panted, tenderly touching her lips, then twisting her lithe body until she sat on the bed facing him, 'a bloody virgin could have managed to last longer than that, and I didn't even come.'

'My, oh my, you really do want the works, don't you.'

He stood up and explored the chest, and discovered a rather nice stainless steel leg-stretcher with a variable width adjustment. He turned his head to where she sat staring at him with that faintly supercilious expression on her face only rich kids manage to achieve with any degree of success.

'Okay, you got it, sunshine,' he announced. 'I'm gonna make those nerve-endings jangle for you like they never jangled before. Ready to say thank you?'

She yanked at the rope around her wrists, her mouth descending into a moue of distaste. 'Fuck off, old man. I've had better than you a thousand times already. Now untie me.'

'What, fed up already?' he said, his light words betraying faint irritation. The damn girl was ripe for chastising, damn her. Except there was no way he was going to get it up for a while now. Hell, he'd get her ready and she could damn well wait for him.

He advanced on her with the leg-stretcher, and she instantly flew into action, kicking with a force which would have downed him had he not been expecting it. He thrust her onto the bed again so he could sit on her bum while he efficiently strapped the implement to her ankles before stretching her legs accommodatingly wide and securing them there.

Going back to the chest he pulled out another stretcher, and once again sitting astride her managed, with very few scratches, to get her wrists untied and secured to the bar. Then he lifted her bodily and carried her to the beam where the electric pulley was waiting, and attached its hook to the centre of the wrist-stretcher before walking over to the electric pulley to wind the contraption up until she stood on tiptoe.

'That good, darling?' he said.

'Could be better,' she snapped. 'Not very original, is it?'

'Patience, dear girl,' he replied. 'We've got plenty of time. Now, just let me slip this nice little hood on for you. Anticipation is a marvellous aphrodisiac.'

'I don't like hoods,' she snarled.

'Getting a little fainthearted, are we?'

Her eyes darted daggers at him and she tried to lash out with her feet, but the stretcher made it impossible for her to achieve any level of accuracy or strength. Kevin advanced with the rubber hood stretched between his hands. 'Open wide, my dear. This one has a nice pump-up gag, which is just up your street.'

He made a fist and stuck a single finger up at her. 'This is your fail-safe sign, d'you understand? You do this to me and I'll stop whatever I'm doing, instantly. But if you do that, I'll go home and that will be the end of it. Now, let's see what you're made of, you rich-bitch cow.'

'What the hell do I need a fail-safe for?' she challenged aggressively. 'I've never needed one before, arsehole.'

'I doubt anyone's ever given you the thrashing you deserve, either, bitch.'

She quivered with excitement. 'You're going to thrash me?'

'I'm going to do what daddy should have done ages ago. I'm going to mark this lovely white bottom with red lines that criss-cross each other, and I'm going to do lots of other things I will thoroughly enjoy. Then when you're really sore I'm going to have sex with you any way which pleases me, and I don't care if you never come. Do you understand?'

He could see she did from the way her eyes began to glaze.

He forced the hood over her head, pushed the gag into her mouth, and pulled the laces tightly down the back, trapping her into darkness and silence. He ran a hand up beneath her skirt, feeling the dampness of his previous loving between her legs, and felt her quiver with anticipation. She was certainly a nubile sexpot. He moved between her accommodating legs and rubbed himself against her, just for the pleasure of being able to do so.

'Right, let's get you naked, Louise, and have a good gander at what you've got to offer.' Discovering a pair of scissors lying on her dressing table, he began slowly, and with great enjoyment, to remove her clothes. She was distinctly unhappy about this arrangement, and made it clear by the grunting noises of discontent that she didn't approve of her designer-ripped clothes being mutilated by the hand of an amateur. However, she did not give him the finger, so he carried on until she was standing there stretched into a wide St Andrew's cross, wearing nothing but her creamy-white birthday suit, with her firm buttocks and ample breasts jutting enticingly.

He cupped those breasts in his hands, weighing them with enjoyment, then slid to the nipples and began to roll them between thumb and forefinger. She moved slightly in time with him, her hips echoing the speed, then jerked as the pressure increased. He noticed her stomach pull in, her chest rise as he carried on twisting, harder and harder, turning the brown teats into barley sugar sticks, one way, then the other way. When he finally let go they were almost twice the size they had been initially, infused with blood.

He ran a finger down her side, from armpit to thigh, and as he stroked her skin seemed to crawl before him, sensitised beyond anything he had ever seen before. From the way she was moving, the way her hands clenched and stretched, he realised she was ready for sex, that her body was in the throes of heightened enjoyment. Not that he was ready to play again. It was easy for a woman; she just had to be a receptacle. The man, however, had to manage an erection, and that was just not possible so soon after shooting his load. But he knew confidently that it would come back. He wasn't too bothered about the wait, and she, after all, had no choice.

He slipped away from her and deftly removed his own clothes. He now knew what Louise wanted, for whatever reason: domination and pain, pure and simple. That anyone could actually desire or be aroused by pain was a new concept for him. It was something he had always fervently believed only existed between the pages of books, and in his own twisted imagination, yet here it was, in the flesh. His own experience with his fantasy woman, so real he could almost taste it, had confirmed this exciting knowledge to his own flesh. Pain and lack of physical control over its delivery were stimulating to the nth degree. Though Kevin was already stimulated simply by the excitement of the situation, he didn't want to hurry. He wanted to linger and wallow in pleasure while he hurt her, for only in his darkest dreams had he ever expected to find a woman in need of this kind of domination. He had never, in his whole and varied sexual career to date, expected to be presented with one in the flesh. Even the thought sent a small and pleasing signal to his prick, making him shiver with exhilaration.

She waited, hanging there, for him to use. He could sense her tension, her expectation, though he had not touched her again. He wandered over to the window, let the blinds up a bit, and sipped his drink, watching the sun highlight her body as life went on in ignorant bliss outside. He knew she listened to the sound of his movements, and was absolutely aware of herself and him, and their intertwined roles.

When ready he carefully put his empty glass down and,

moving silently like a prowling animal, chose from her chest a whippy riding crop. He bent it between his hands as he imagined her going into a shop to purchase it, secretly excited, while on the surface appearing bland and unconcerned and the owner of recalcitrant horses.

He reached out, touched her between the legs with the tip of the crop. She jolted ferociously. His lips drew back in a wolfish smile. He pulled his wrist back and aimed not for the buttocks as she would be anticipating, but for the tip of one breast. The crop hit the bloated nipple with a crack, instantly leaving a fine red line on either side. Louise jerked with a cry of astonishment, her body leaping upward in a co-ordinated movement which would have made a gymnast happy. Then her feet regained the floor, and she stood, tensed, waiting for the next slash, panting heavily behind the mask. Kevin smiled and waited, watching her head tilt slightly as she struggled to hear. Only when she began to fidget with unrest did he draw back his wrist to aim another shot, this time on the inside of one white thigh.

Again she lurched with a shot of pleasure which was almost equalled by a response from his own body. So soon? he thought. Well, well. Now his prick attained a pendulous appearance, and to assist in his own enjoyment he wrapped a cord around his balls and tied it off. Almost instantly little signals of desire flashed through to his brain, matched with the pulsing spasms of his own sexual constriction. He raised his arm and the crop flashed again and again until her breasts were crossed with fine red lines and she was scrabbling round and round in a circle to escape the instrument wreaking torment upon her body.

Yet although her hands were working and flexing, still she did not give him the finger.

He moved close, held her against his nakedness, and felt the tip of his prick touch the warmth of her vagina. He groaned with the flooding sensation that accompanied it, and pressed his face to her heaving breasts. 'Had enough, Louise?' he grunted. 'You want me to go away?'

A stifled groan came from behind the black mask and she shuddered, trying unsuccessfully to mount him in spite of her bonds. He held her still with his hands around her ribcage, and bent slightly to suck at one sore teat, his tongue rasping over the ridges and circling the lump of flesh around and around. Then he took a deep breath, sucked as much of the delightful mammary into his mouth as hard as he could, milking it with his lips until he was gasping for breath, and then released it with a plop.

This action satisfactory, he repeated it on the other breast, sensing her grow more and more tense as the pressure built up in his mouth, enjoying the way her whole body echoed the explosive release of tension.

Moving behind her, Kevin then began to rub up and down, knowing he was nearly ready. He knew what he wanted. He stuffed his finger up inside her where the juices flowed, hot and strong, then using her own lubricant he inserted his finger into her anus. She jolted with shock, tightened around his finger with incredible force. But he sensed that was what she wanted. He repeated the action several times until his finger glided in and out easily, then lifted her up and back until her arse was almost sitting on him.

Now his cock was proudly rampant, hard as a rock, and

if he had been looking he would have seen his balls as fiery red suns, separated by the string that was constricting them. All he knew was that it felt wonderful – second to nothing at all. With his hands around her thighs he held her there and gradually let her weight drop onto his prick. Her arse felt the heat of him, and pulsed as her own body weight gradually, inexorably, sank her down onto that ready shaft, her spread legs allowing him total access.

When she was fully impaled he began to move, just slightly. He pulled her body back into his and rubbed her breasts, her thighs, letting her hang there, her ring pulsing against the fullness of him. He groaned and bit into her shoulder, and he heard her gasping with flooding sensations over which she had no control. Very, very gently, he began to masturbate her.

She shuddered with uncontrollable urges as he rubbed faster and faster, until eventually he felt the tiny fluctuation that was the onset of her orgasm. He held his finger still, feeling the heat radiate through her from the core of her body.

Surprised at the sheer ferocity of that orgasm Kevin could hold back no longer. He bent his knees and began to grind up and down the tight constriction of her bottom until the heat became a burning fire in his balls which exploded upward like a geyser inside her. Then with a sigh of satisfaction and sheer exhaustion he pulled out and flopped onto his back on the bed.

He turned his head. Louise hung there, shifting faintly with discomfort, the marks on her body flaming against her white skin, still not crying pax. Putting his hands behind his head, Kevin just lay and watched her with enjoyment, she was so incredibly beautiful.

When he was sufficiently rested he went and examined her chest of wonderful toys once more. To his delight he found things he had only ever seen in catalogues, and over the next couple of hours managed to bring himself to orgasm twice more until he collapsed, exhausted.

After showering he released Louise from her bonds and lifted the rubber hood from her flushed face. She looked disorientated, spaced out, and as tired as he was. He smacked her bum, making her wince. 'Bed,' he said, and she went obediently without a word, burned out by the internal fires he had stoked.

He awoke in the morning refreshed enough to thrust himself into her with little finesse, before leaving.

Looking forward to Esther's tender ministrations once more, Kevin laboured under the happy knowledge that what he had done was for all for her. She was a lady, not like Louise, and it was far far better that he kept his more animal instincts and his dark desires where they belonged – out of her sight.

Chapter Eight

When Kevin got home, his clothes infused with the smoky scent of josticks, Esther said nothing, although she noticed the tiredness in his face and heard the lies in his voice. Yet she was not as upset as she would have been a few months ago. She played the dutiful wife for the rest of the day, lulling him into complacency and stroking his ego. She plied him with wine and rubbed his feet with massage oils, amused by the fact that this erotic action engendered not the slightest bit of interest in her husband. Oh, had he been having himself a good time.

Later that night, once she heard Kevin's breathing subside to a slow and laborious snore she climbed out of bed and turned on the light. He wouldn't wake. She was euphoric. She was walking on air. Until you experience it, Madam had said, you will not understand. Experience what? she had asked, confused, thinking Madam meant some kinky kind of sexual act.

Madam meant self-confidence, and with it the glorious freedom to enjoy life with uninhibited pleasure. Esther discovered this elusive thing had not arrived in a blinding flash, but grew inside her so slowly and insidiously she had not even noticed its arrival, but once she did, she knew it was with her forever. It was that indefinable thing which separated people into leaders and followers, doers and whiners. It blossomed deep inside the psyche, and was enhanced only by the realisation that to be interested in self was not selfishness so much as awareness.

She learned that lesson more fully than she realised on the night of the business dinner. That evening changed her perception of self more fully than Madam or Kevin could know, for nothing was visible to the eye. Yet she thrived on the memory. For the first time in her life she had walked into a crowded room and every eye there turned to her. The deliberate sexual magnetism of her attire had made her feel wonderful; the women stared with an admiration born of jealousy, the men with lust. There was power! She had enjoyed every moment. Even to the jealousy in her husband's eyes. Especially that.

He had not displayed jealousy since before their marriage. It seemed a very long time, yet within an hour she had men grovelling for her attention, and their wives, perforce, were begging for her favours. She knew those who had pitied her before were jealous now, but if there was a sex symbol orbiting in their vicinity, they wanted to control access. She had wanted to laugh out loud!

How Kevin had revelled in those long-awaited invitations. And how she had enjoyed being the catalyst that finally made it happen. The truth was awesome. Now she knew what they meant by behind every powerful man is a powerful woman. Men were so driven by their pricks, by their inherent superiority, they didn't realise women were just as strong, but in a more devious fashion, and they just couldn't accept that women had the same force driving them when it was disguised by femininity. The only difference Esther could see was that women had the strength to manipulate that sexual drive instead of allowing it to dictate to them.

She hummed to herself as she wrapped the thick leather straps around her husband's wrists. She saw him smile through his drugged sleep as she trussed him, and she loved him more than she had in a long time. Then she pushed him onto his back and climbed over him. 'Enjoy,' she whispered, holding his hands above his head, and felt his sex move feebly in response to her slow kiss. It was nice to be in charge.

Then she went to sleep.

Some time later Kevin awoke to the feel of leather restraints around his wrist and ankles. He tested their strength happily. Oh, boy, he thought as he found them immovable. Oh, boy. As his head began to pound with the expected hangover he realised he was stretched between two points, wrists crossed above his head, ankles spread wide and trussed tightly.

He wriggled experimentally. He was racked tightly on a soft surface. A bed. Yes, that made sense. The confinement and the connotations immediately sent signals to his sexual awareness, and he wallowed in the lonely enjoyment of his predicament. He wanted to touch himself, and it was unbelievably erotic not to be able to do so. He waited, knowing that *she* was behind it; that *she* would arrive at some stage and do wonderful things to him – things he had barely hoped could ever happen. He was undeniably out of control of his present situation, and though he writhed and tested the bonds again and again, escape was very far from his present desires.

The confinement was exquisite.

Welcome, dream woman, he thought, afraid to open his

eyes in case this sexual euphoria disappeared.

And suddenly she was there. A waft of exotic scent, the sensuous touch of a fingertip upon his bare skin. He moaned in anticipation.

'What shall I do, I wonder?' she whispered.

'Fuck me,' Kevin replied hopefully, eyes tightly shut in case she disappeared with awakening. 'Fuck the pants off of me.'

'Tut-tut, such a lack of finesse. Fucking undoubtedly will happen, but what shall I do first? Shall I gag you? Shall I beat you? Shall I give you a massage? Tell me, slave. What shall it be?'

'Beat me,' he said softly, feeling the exquisite shiver of excitement fill him at the thought. 'Please beat me, mistress. I've had thoughts about you beating me which have been driving me to distraction because I thought I'd never see you again.'

'You're not seeing me now, slave. Do you mind?'

Her voice was soft, sensuous, and oh so sexy. 'No, mistress,' he croaked. He felt the soft touch of leather around his eyes and knew he was safely blindfolded. He tried to open his eyes, and could not. The relief! 'Chastise me, goddess,' he whispered, and writhed in the darkness of his fantasy.

'What did you call me?' She was astonished.

'Goddess,' he repeated urgently. 'Queen of my darkest fantasies, chastise me!'

Blimey, thought Esther, staring at her bound and erect husband. Now what? She took the new leather bondage straps she had bought and wrapped them about his body. Around his chest, middle, thighs, and knees, not adding to his confinement, for he could not move, but binding him more deeply into his own sexual awareness.

Then she sat and watched while he writhed, enjoying his confinement, locked into some private eroticism the bondage alone stimulated. His penis pulsed, and she had to do nothing, for he was pleasing himself with his thoughts. 'You dirty old man,' she said to herself in amusement, and began to knead her own flesh in response to a sudden overpowering urge from within.

After a while the simple confinement began to pall, though, and Kevin began to make dissatisfied noises. 'You want me to touch you, slave?' Esther whispered.

'Yes, oh yes,' he groaned.

She reached out and stroked the bonds at his wrists. 'You're not going to be silly and try to escape, are you, slave?'

'No,' he groaned. 'Oh, no.'

She released his ankles from the end of the bed, then unbuckled one restrained wrist. 'Roll over,' she ordered.

Dutifully he did so and let her twist his free arm behind his back and clip his wrist into the thick waist belt.

'And the other one,' she continued, and the other wrist followed suit.

She sat back on her heels and watched her husband for a moment, bemused by the power she had over him. He could have escaped at that moment, had he wanted to. Obviously he did not. Now, however, his wrists were firmly affixed to his spine. She joined his ankles with a six-inch strap, then made him sit up.

'Walk,' she ordered.

'Where to, mistress?' he asked humbly, attaining his

feet, but finding balance slightly difficult.

'Forward,' she told him, and gave him a smart rap on the buttocks. When they reached the stairs she instructed, 'Now step down. One, two, three...'

He edged forward, one step at a time. 'Where are you taking me?' he asked. 'Where am I?'

Questions tinged with excitement and fear.

'To my dungeon, slave,' she said.

'And what will you do to me there?'

He was positively quivering with excitement, she realised. It was certainly not fear.

'What would you like me to do?' she mused. 'Shall you be a schoolgirl who needs spanking, perhaps, and I the teacher? Maybe you're in a mental hospital, wrapped in a straightjacket and about to have electric treatment to stop your terrible wanking? Or perhaps I am the gangster's moll with a gun to your head while you lick my shoes clean? Or perhaps you're the prisoner and I the torturer encased in skin-tight rubber? Or maybe you like my leather and whips?' Each time she adjusted her voice to suit the character, and he shuffled determinedly down the hall before her to the altered garage.

'I am your prisoner, fair torturer,' he said hoarsely. 'I can see you. You're wearing studded leather and high-heeled shoes and you're carrying a whip. I'm quivering at your feet, goddess.'

'Then shall I whip you and make you pay for your infidelity, slave?'

His imagination had taken over entirely. 'Please,' he begged, stumbling forward as fast as his hobbles would permit. 'Please!'

'And how shall I whip you?' she teased. 'On the wooden cross, on tiptoe with your arms stretched, or across the horse with your backside bare? Or shall I merely chain you to the bars of your cell?'

He groaned with pleasure. 'Anything you wish, mistress. Anything!'

'And you've been so very wicked, haven't you, slave? You've been enjoying yourself with another, after all I told you before.'

'I have been so very wicked, mistress. Very, very wicked.'

For a moment Esther wondered whether to ask him who he'd been wicked with, but decided that perhaps she would rather not know. He would know what he was being punished for, and would no doubt tell her when he thought he'd been punished enough. Then she would decide whether or not to stop.

'Very well, I grant your wish,' she went on. 'You will be punished for your wickedness, slave. I shall beat you until your flesh screams. I shall whip you until there is not an inch of flesh left unpunished.'

'Yes please, mistress,' he agreed hoarsely, and groaned with anticipation as he was thrust hard against the cold metal bars of his cell. She pulled a collar around his neck and clipped it to the bars, pulling him in so that his face pressed into the cold steel.

'You've been very wicked,' Esther said softly, 'and I must punish you severely. Do you know why?'

'Because I've been with another woman, mistress?'

'Not because you've been with another woman, slave, but because you felt you needed to. Anything she can do,

I can do better. Anything you did to her, you should do to me – if I let you. I am the only woman in your life from now on. The only woman. You will learn that.'

'But this is not—' He was about to explain about his wife, when the words were plugged abruptly as she thrust a thick wedge of leather between his teeth, which forced his jaws apart and pulled his lips back in the parody of a smile. This was not comfortable in the least, and he had not finished saying what he wanted to say, but she ignored his muffled grumbles and proceeded to tighten straps over the top and back of his head, keeping the gag in place.

Suddenly Kevin wasn't quite so sure he liked the idea. He was too vulnerable. Suddenly the idea of extreme punishment didn't seem quite so desirable. Hell, what was he thinking of, damn it? Unable to voice his sudden misgiving, he pulled determinedly at the cuffs around his wrists, deciding that enough was enough.

Esther stood back and watched for a moment. Gone was the passive acceptance. He had slipped into the resistive mode. Madam had taught her about that; about the time when notions of propriety and society warred against the calls of the flesh. Now she would have to be careful. The bars to which he was attached were not, in fact, part of a cell, but were a square grill attached firmly to floor and ceiling, and placed at ninety degrees to the wall of what had once been the garage. But it was well concreted in.

She walked to the other side of the grill, threaded a rope through it and pulled his knees tightly to the bars, forestalling movement. Then she was able to attach two ropes to the ankle cuffs, and a further two to his wrist cuffs, carefully avoiding the urgently groping fingers that tried desperately to stop her. Then she released the temporary rope around his knees and, to his extreme annoyance, pulled and separated his ankles as far as they would comfortably spread and tied them off.

Then she took a firm hold of one rope that threaded through the bars, and released each wrist in turn. Before he knew what was happening he was spread-eagled, struggling and grunting, against the bars.

Oh, God, Kevin thought, feeling a chill air reach his balls and arse. Once again, thrills of fear and anticipation raged through his body, and his cock began to pump up with familiar urgency. He listened. What was she doing? He tensed. He remembered the whip.

But no. Soft oiled hands began to smooth all over his body, to rub and touch his electrified skin. He could feel naked tits against his back. He groaned and his hips began to move. Her soft hands glided, teased, and then they were between his legs, possessing his sensitised cock and balls. He gripped the bars and groaned, his rampant erection pulsing in her grip.

Then she was gone.

No, she was still there, the hands were back. They were wrapping something round and round his cock, tighter and tighter. There was an awful stretched feeling, then the hands left him. He moved experimentally, gasped, and was still. Movement was pain. Beautifully erotic pain. His cock was threatening to explode with the tightness of the bindings that pulled his hips hard into the bars and held him totally immobile.

He held his breath, listened.

Again she was behind him. She was kneeling between

his stretched legs, and was running oiled hands up and down his inner thighs – up and down, up and down, closer and closer to his exposed arse.

He shuddered with anticipation. Such unbelievable eroticism; the feel of her hands upon his skin, the confinement of his organs and his total inability to move, to escape, or even to complain. Without warning a finger slipped into his arse, causing him to buck with shock. Then that finger began to glide in and out, the motion of his anus contracting and stretching further pumping his crucified balls into agonising stimulation.

Then, as if that were not enough, the finger was withdrawn, and something else pressed hard against him, pushed inexorably in until his oiled anus opened obligingly to give it access. He felt her fiddling with the restraint around his middle, and whatever she had pushed into him was now confined there by more straps. The stretched, alien sensation was incredible. It couldn't be more strange and lovely; until it began to buzz. His limbs pulsed involuntarily as spasms of sexual fire ran through him, starting deep in his bowels and rolling outward to his extremities in hot waves.

At that point Esther left her husband to enjoy himself. She changed into the new leather suit she had bought, donned the high-heeled ankle boots, and covered face and hair with a fitted leather hood.

When she went back Kevin was moaning softly. His penis was flacid now, relieving the tension in his body.

She removed his blindfold.

For a moment Kevin blinked in the harsh light. As his eyes came into focus he became aware of her standing before him, framed by the black metal bars which confined him. She was a goddess and torturer. Her face was concealed, but her breasts were perfect orbs supported by a clever array of leather straps. Her feet were encased in high-heeled ankle boots which were placed wide, causing her thigh and calf muscles to tense in shapely beauty. And between her black-gloved hands she bent a long leather whip.

Kevin shivered.

She walked forward and knelt.

Kevin tried to look down, but with the collar clamped to the bars, could not move far enough to see what she was doing.

'Is that nice, slave?' she teased, rubbing him back to full erection. 'Now I'm going to start hurting you. This is going to be so nice. Are you ready?'

He made guttural noises of discontent.

'What, not happy?' She stood.

He tried to make her aware that enough was enough. She reached for his face and pulled two clips from the side of the gag and fixed them to the bars, keeping him looking firmly to the front.

'Nnnng!' he complained as she sank down from view again, and he tensed expectantly.

'I am going to so enjoy this, slave,' she murmured softly, her words an endearment, her fingers reaching around him, tracing small circles on his buttocks as if searching out targets to aim for.

Kevin bucked against the bars. No, no, he didn't want to be beaten after all. Not really. Not at all! It was not too late to change his mind, please? But as she reached up through the bars and began to rub his nipples between her fingers, rubbing, rolling, pulling, until they began to burn, he knew even if he could speak, he would simply beg for more. The action hovered between pain and pleasure, sending sharp signals to his prick, which throbbed accordingly.

Very soon Kevin was lost in his involuntary world of sex, and was merely a body fed tantalising promises by a siren in black leather. She was a fucking nympho, he thought.

Then she was gone.

He tried to look round, but could not, and stared in agonised anticipation at the bare white wall before him. He felt soft hands reach round, pinch his sore nipples once more, and then retreat.

He waited...

What the hell? That strange sensation around his nipples was not fingers. It was something mechanical, and seemed to get tighter and tighter by the second, but he could not look down to discover what she had done. He writhed for a moment, fighting the new and strange confinement that was making his nipples pulse so frantically. He moaned, struggled, and whimpered, self-pity mixed up with a sort of self-loathing because the confinement was so erotically pleasing, and surely a man wasn't supposed to be pleased at being used in such a dastardly way?

But she was touching him all over, pressing into his back, agitating the vibrator that filled his back passage. Simply having her playing with him pumped him up to pleasing fullness, jammed into the tightness of the bindings. He wriggled slightly, felt everything move and pull. He groaned at the self-induced discomfort, and moved some more. Oh, it was lovely...

He heard the faint whistle of the whip a fraction of a second before it landed. He wailed. The whip bit across both buttocks with unerring accuracy, stealing his breath and cutting him off mid-scream. As he rebounded against the pain the cord tightened around his cock and balls. He squealed, gasped against the flood of sensations. He struggled against his bonds, gurgling furiously, but the more he struggled the more the cord pleased him, bringing him to rock hard erection against the rope's confinement.

'You want to say something to me, slave?'

He grunted his affirmative. She removed the gag. He spat the leather out.

'Do you want me to stop?' his fair tormentor whispered, in a voice which dripped sex.

'No,' he groaned, while another part of his mind wondered what the hell he was saying. 'Please... more...'

He sensed her raise the whip again. He heard the whistle, tensed, gritted his teeth, and bucked as it landed across his thighs. 'Oh...' he groaned.

Again the whip fell.

'More?' she goaded.

'Yes, mistress,' he gasped.

Esther beat her husband until his buttocks were a glowing mass of pulsing red stripes and his penis was a purple brand tipped with a glowing coal stoking the air through the bars. She hit him until her own sex was dripping with need, her body flushed with desire, her breath short with lust. Then, with hasty fingers, she released his bonds. Twisting him around in the hasty parody of a waltz, she grasped the bars above her head, opening her body invitingly. Kevin was hardly aware of what he was doing as he lifted her legs and thrust his way into the exposed accommodation just once, twice, thrice, before he came with a fantastic and painful orgasm.

Only when he was finished did he realise that he was free. He stared at her, and lowered her feet to the floor.

They stared into each other's eyes. She was at his mercy now; he could rip her hood off...

He backed away, suddenly afraid. This was no dream. How he got here he didn't know, but he was afraid to look. Afraid he would leave his wife for this woman, this sexual animal who could command him to do anything she wanted, and he would obey. He didn't want to see her face. He didn't want to know who had tied him, beaten, him, and given him the best sexual ride he'd had in a long time, because he was afraid he would lose her. Or lose his marriage. Or lose himself.

'Slave, there is some wine on the table,' the beautiful siren said. 'Drink it.'

He knew it would be drugged.

Chapter Nine

Esther stared at her sleeping husband, now back in their bed. He would wake up the next day with no idea how he had got there, and she had to carry on playing the simple wife who did not know he had been up to anything unusual.

She pursed her lips pensively. The game was progressing just how Madam Tisset had said it would. She had found Kevin's trigger, all right. She smiled at the thought. Who would have thought the Casanova of the banking world was entertaining secret dreams of being dominated by a woman wielding a whip? Those items had merely been her own choice, her way of forcing his darkest fantasies out of him. Perhaps they had more in common than either of them had realised.

She nursed a small measure of relief that she had not discovered his fetish to be something she could not handle. At least his dreams of domination were easily satisfied, and his secret sexual desires compatible with the imposed boundaries of their marriage. And if she kept it up, then he would have neither the time nor the inclination to keep ploughing new turf out of his own domain. But she could not keep up the pretence indefinitely. It was just not possible, even though she was pleased with the effectiveness of her disguised voice. She glanced at the mirror and, behind the obvious tiredness, recognised that the woman who stared back was still obviously not happy.

Kevin turned over and snored. She smiled faintly at his innocent sleeping face, wondering how he was going to explain his weal-marked buttocks to the innocent wife. On reflection, however, she doubted he would even need to try. After all, they dressed in the dark and made love in the dark.

Except for that time in the hall.

She grew warm with the memory. Why could he not just let go with her more often? God, that had been good. She grimaced, he had not even recognised her orgasm when it had arrived, assuming that his virtual rape had hurt her. What an idiot! But then, so had she been for so long. Hemmed in by convention, by fear of being wanton. Sex was so much better than she had ever realised it could be. But it was still not enough. Kevin had fucked her out of his own necessity; a need brought on by anger, pique, jealousy – all sorts of reasons. But not for the one she wanted him to experience; the desire to please her equally.

In spite of his recent ordeals, he was still being very superior and condescending. She thought of the earrings he had bought her, and knew what it meant when people talked about grinding their teeth. Had all the other little trinkets he had given her over the three years of their marriage been out of guilt? If so, he had well and truly played the field while she had remained in virtual ignorance. What a fool she had been! And what an insensitive bastard he'd been, pleasing all those other women, and not the one that mattered.

Fingers curled into claws, reached towards him slightly, but with an effort she relaxed. Madam Tisset had been wrong in one respect; it was not just his fault, they had both been at fault. They had fallen into their roles in the marriage with serious lack of thought and total commitment to Victorian ideals. God, she had even been married in white, like a virgin. Barring the broken hymen, she might well have been one for all she knew about sex. How innocent she had been!

She had supposed that lying on her back and thinking of England was enough, because that was all Kevin demanded. And she guessed he had thought her happy to be the wife his Victorian upbringing had led him to expect. In his defence, she mused, he probably really did want his wife to be a 'nice' girl, because a nice girl would not play around. If she had acted like a bitch in heat in the early days of their marriage, he probably would have assumed she was being as unfaithful as he was, and that would have finished the marriage before it had a chance. She knew that in spite of living in the twentieth century, Kevin did cherish the rather quaint notion that it was acceptable for men to be unfaithful, but not women. Where did the men think the women they bonked came from? Outer space?

What he had to be made to realise was that both his home comforts and his sexual desires could be satisfied by his own wife. And the other part of that realisation was of that he had to be made aware of her needs, to realise that she was a red-blooded woman, and that it was not bad to be so. Otherwise, one day she might really become a bitch in heat, go off looking for satisfaction from some other man instead of just doing it in her dreams.

But how?

Kevin was so complacent he simply could not accept that homely little Esther had a burning need to see her sexual fantasies enacted. He probably didn't even think she had fantasies. And if she did, he probably thought he was them. Arrogant prick! Yet she knew she was being unkind in her thoughts. It had taken someone else to teach her that dreams and fantasies were not necessarily wrong. It had also taken a lot more soul-searching to find the strength of mind to put these new thoughts into action.

She smiled, lay back and closed her eyes. If he was not capable of thinking it out on his own, she would have to do it for him – but now was not the time. With the ease of long practice, to satisfy her own lustful cravings, she turned her drifting thoughts to a normal morning, to seeing Kevin off with a wave of the hand before turning to face her empty house.

This was her own private dream; that the hallway was not empty.

As she closed the door behind her, to her shock she realised there was a man dressed in scruffy jeans and a checked shirt wedged behind it. She stared for a brief moment before opening her mouth to scream. The stranger leapt forward, rammed a hand over her mouth and pulled her into the curve of his body with his other hand. She reached up, whimpering, to scrabble instinctively at the ridges of muscle which confined her.

'Keep still!' he commanded harshly. 'I don't want to hurt to you.'

She turned to stone and froze compliantly in his arms at the implied threat. He sidled to the kitchen window, and she went with him, feet scrabbling for purchase, the whites of her eyes gleaming up at the chiselled beauty of his face. He pulled back the net curtain a fraction. Locked in an unloving embrace, they both watched. The road was still. Eventually she felt his body relax.

'It seems I've lost them. Now, if I take my hand away do you promise not to scream?'

After a second she nodded. Did she have any choice? He moved his hand away fraction, tensed at her indrawn breath, then released her save for a hand on one shoulder. He indicated a small kitchen chair. 'Sit down. Push the chair right in and put your hands on the table.'

'What are you—?'

Blue eyes inflicted a warning, stilled her tongue. 'I've just escaped, and I'm not about to give myself up without a fight. Does that scare you?'

'Yes,' she said honestly.

'Good.'

He continued to watch the road with hawk-like ferocity while she sat there, hands on the table as she'd been told, watching him. He was not a large man, but compact, lithe, his whole body tense and volatile as if waiting to explode into action. There was a primitive beauty about him, something wild and untamed, not at all what she was used to in her own socially-aware husband. With a faint shiver of something tantalising, she saw the way his tight jeans moulded against his thighs and recalled the way his rock-hard chest had pressed against her.

They were a still tableau for a while, he at the window, she at the table. Then gradually he relaxed, turned to face her, and drawled, 'Well, it seems I did lose them, after all. That's nice, isn't it?'

He leaned against the sink, crossing bronzed forearms across his chest. Above them a sprinkling of dark curly hair escaped his unbuttoned shirt. He had a sort of careless grace, with his brilliant blue eyes, and slightly unkempt hair, but she was not deceived. This man was a criminal, desperate to remain at large.

Then, to her horror she saw a dawning interest in their situation in his gaze, and realised his eyes began to assess her with new awareness. 'I think I would be wise to stay here for a while,' he commented, amusement touching his eyes at her comprehension.

She flushed, fleetingly touching her fingertips to a slightly bruised lip. 'My husband—'

'Will not return till after five, darling,' he interrupted confidently. 'True?'

She nodded, then it was too late to lie.

His lazy gaze stripped her. 'Then we have plenty of time to get to know each other better before I have to leave.'

'I – I can't,' she whispered. 'My husband—'

'Isn't here – I am. And besides, you have no choice.' He crossed the gap between them in two easy strides and took a firm handful of her hair. He twisted insistently, turning her face up to his, and gazed into her eyes as he lifted her to her feet. The chair squeaked back along the tiled floor. She was pulled into a close embrace, his chest smothering her soft breasts, then his lips pressed on hers.

She pushed ineffectually at him, but his hand knotted a little tighter in her hair, bringing tears to her eyes. He drew back a fraction. 'I like my women to respond,' he warned, his breath a warm whisper on her lips.

Fearfully she opened her mouth, and responded to his

kiss with something less than enthusiasm. It seemed to satisfy him, though. His other hand crept around her back, pressing her tightly to him, leaving her in no doubt that he was already turned on.

Her own hands fluttered against his hips, then grasped his shirt as he pulled her off balance.

'Pull my shirt out,' he commanded, his tongue lapping her lips between words. 'I want to feel your hands on me.'

Shocked to quivering compliance, she tugged obediently at the fabric, and then whispered back, 'I can't. It's too tight.'

'Then undo my jeans.'

She fumbled with the heavy fabric, the dark-treacle promise in his voice sending waves of desire to her very core. She undid the button, then slid the zipper down. He groaned deep in his throat as her hands brushed up against the huge lump in his trousers and managed to pull his shirt free. Her fingers slid up the taut skin beneath to discover he truly was as muscular as he had seemed, all lean whipcord strength. She wondered what the police wanted him for, but didn't wonder anything very much after that, because he was now moving against her with a building intensity. He ripped her blouse from her waistband, reached inside to undo her bra, then his hand was pressing and circling the mound of flesh, rolling the tight nipple between brutish fingers. She gasped, but could say nothing because his tongue was invading her mouth, his lips possessing hers, silencing any complaints she may have felt obliged to a utter.

Then his hand slid down, pushed inside her skirt and pants to encompass one firm buttock. Panicked, she put her hands against his chest and tried to push away, but it was like pushing at a brick wall. Nothing bent beneath her frantic efforts. Suddenly his softness was gone. He swore, turned her around suddenly, heaved her clothes down over her hips and pushed to her face against the kitchen table, the one hand holding her there, the other clumsy with haste as he tugged her clothes down to her ankles and ripped them off. Her blouse he pulled up savagely and left there, tangling her arms in a knot above her head.

Then, as quickly as it started, his violence was gone. 'Oh, you're beautiful,' he grunted. One hand, more gentle now, held her by the neck, forestalling movement, while the other caressed the white lengths of her back, sending crazy signals of anger and desire to the very core of her sex. The hand slid inexorably towards the crease between her full buttocks, dwelt in tantalising pleasure for a moment on her anus, and then slipped further to separate and lubricate the thickened lips below.

She lay there across the table, her useless hands trapped by fabric, her cheek pressed to the scrubbed pine table, unable to do more than accept; for although conscience told her to struggle, he had awakened in her a desire of the same intensity as his own. A jeans-clad knee inserted itself between her legs, opening her more fully for his pleasure, making her available for his use. His hands left her body for a moment, and she shuddered as the fabric of his own clothes scraped past her inner thighs, letting her feel the heat of his bare skin. He leaned down, kissed her shoulder, and murmured, 'You'll enjoy this. I know you will, you sexy whore,' and he pushed his throbbing organ against the lubricated lips of her vagina. She felt the heat of him pressing, opening her for his pleasure, and her body sucked him in greedily, aroused by his forceful actions. Holding her firmly by the shoulders he began to work himself backwards and forwards, pleasing himself with slow and indulgent strokes.

At first she lay acquiescent, determined not to encourage him, but she could no longer hold back. Groaning deep in her throat, Esther began to move in unison with the muscled stranger. The unexpected response fired him to new enthusiasm, and with the violence of mutual need, he began to thrust to a climax within her captive body. Finding her recumbent position on the table hindering his access, he released her shoulders to lift her hips, the better to accommodate his urgent erection. As he pounded against her she was brought to her own peak, and even as he ejaculated with a triumphant roar, so did she. There was a moment of union, of exhausted silence and drawn breath before he withdrew with a faint curse of sated lust.

Esther made to move, but he forestalled her. Holding her still with one heavy hand he ripped the remains of her clothes from her, then pulled her to her feet, letting her know in no uncertain terms who was in charge.

'No,' he grunted, 'show me the bathroom. That was a nice little aperitif. Give me a few more moments and I'll come up with the main course. And if you're a really good girl, we'll have a sweet before I bid you farewell. This is as good a place as I can think of to sit tight and wait for the evening.'

'But I—'

'Shut up! Women always talk and spoil things.' He

pulled her through the living room and towards the stairs, his eyes roving, searching – for what she did not know. He dragged her into the bathroom, but washing was not on his mind. Not releasing the tight grip he had on her upper arm, he began to throw open cupboards and rifle through pots and jars. Eventually he gave a crow of delight. 'Ha! I knew I'd find it: a fine, well-stocked emergency bag. What woman doesn't have one?'

Esther had dreamed of Kevin finding this bag full of rolls of sticky tape and using it on her, but it took the stranger to do so. As he removed the bag from under the sink she felt a tremor of excitement. What was he going to do to her next?

He turned her violently and began to bind her elbows together behind her back, making her breasts thrust forward under that unnatural stress. She gasped at the sudden movement and pulled involuntarily, but he carried on binding until her forearms and hands were totally encased by white bandage. She pulled at her wrists, and a tremor flitted through her body at the confinement. She was already putty in his hands, but now she felt absolutely vulnerable, exposed, available for whatever he wanted to do.

Her arms safely secured he twisted her around, and with a brief smile, slapped a wide plaster over her mouth. He bent his head and with wicked pleasure kissed the plaster that covered her lips. 'Now they're safe until I want to use them,' he breathed huskily.

Grabbing his booty, he thrust her back down the stairs, and with a brief, sidelong glance at him as they turned at the bottom, Esther saw his penis was already tumescent, and she knew it wouldn't be long before he was fully erect again.

In the living room she was thrust aggressively into a chair while her captor stood before her, gloriously naked, open consideration on his face as he perused her heaving breasts and decided quite what he should do next.

'You're very lovely,' he said eventually, leaning forward to run a hand over one breast. His eyes narrowed slightly as she shivered, and his penis flicked a fraction higher. He growled, a low sound of enjoyment and bent, parting her legs so he could kneel between them. Holding her knees apart he studied her infused labia for a moment, then reached forward to hold her waist and taste one breast, then the other.

Esther's nostrils flared as she breathed deeply, sensitised by the strangeness of his touch and her total vulnerability. But this only made her breasts more available to him, and he slobbered at her flesh avidly. She could neither close her legs or use her hands to protect the nipples he was now feasting upon. The fear of his nipping teeth was an aphrodisiac, sending shivers of delight down her spine, yet her legs involuntarily tightened around his waist, trying to thrust him away.

'No, no,' he whispered. 'Naughty girl. Those toys are mine to touch and play with. You can't stop me, you know.' He bent and nibbled some more. She made weak mewling noises, and her eyes closed a fraction.

Then suddenly he stood and walked into the kitchen.

She stayed where he had put her for just a moment, wondering if she should try to escape, but as the thought crossed her mind the man, all muscle and tan and tattoos came back in carrying her broom. Leering with anticipation, and despite her struggles as comprehension dawned, he took the roll of sticky plaster and easily bound her ankles wide apart to the handle.

'Now try to shut the door on me, you sexy little whore,' he gloated, with evident satisfaction.

A firm hand lifted the horizontal broom, and the other began to play with the exposed damp area between her legs. He watched, never taking his eyes from her face as his hand wreaked havoc on her out of sight. Folded in half, she felt his fingers glide in and out, circle the edges of her orifices, teasing the small nub of her sex, before one was suddenly inserted into her anus. She stiffened and gave a strangled gasp of pleasure, followed by a long sigh of disappointment as the finger exited, and the muscle squeezed closed once more. Oh, why didn't Kevin ever do that? It was so decadent, so beautifully immoral.

The stranger lingered there, groping, touching places surely not designed to be touched, and enjoying her body as though it really was his own personal toy. And yet his enjoyment was not entirely selfish. Although she was bound she sensed he wanted her to enjoy his mastery of her, and knew that the satisfaction in his gaze was partially derived from her inability to control her responses.

Eventually he lifted the bar which parted her legs, rose to his feet, taking his weight on his arms, and leaned his body down to press her almost in half. Once again she felt the heat of his erection press towards her eager sex. He lingered there a while, greasing himself on the juices from her flowing glands, tantalising her by not thrusting in fully. Then his eyes narrowed, she sensed a tension in him, and to her shock felt the white heat of his penis press hard against her exposed anus. She held her breath, and saw a question in his eyes.

Then he pressed harder. Instinct took over. Now he was not smiling; his lips as tense as the muscles in his arms. He pushed, groaned, sank deep inside the tight ring, felt it squeeze the blood-infused cock into luscious expansion, then relax just slightly as he began to ease himself in and out of that slick accommodation. Beads of sweat gleamed on his face as he masturbated in the living doll beneath him, thrusting with more and more urgency as the need to ejaculate consumed him, and was contained by willpower alone.

Then, when he was about to burst, his fingers thrust between her legs and rubbed briefly at the excited nub of sex which was exposed to him. Her orgasm flooded them both, and as her anus clenched around his buried shaft he, too, came.

Eventually reality intruded. Esther's face was flushed with exertion as she realised she still lay next to Kevin, her muscles shaking with tiredness, the dream over. She dragged herself from orgasm to awareness for just long enough to slip the vibrator back into the drawer beside their bed. She had discovered long ago that it was not enough to simply use the gadget. To produce an orgasm of splendid proportions it had to be accompanied by some kind of erotic imagery.

She reflected that she was getting rather good at it.

And while Kevin wallowed in his own dreams beside her, her last conscious thoughts were that the young man who changed tyres at the garage would be rather surprised to find himself the object of her sexual fantasies, followed by a feeling of disappointment that it had not really happened. But at that point, still savouring of the delicious feel of imaginary bindings around her elbows and wrists, and the remnants of a real but self-induced orgasm, Esther drifted off into sleep.

Chapter Ten

Kevin awoke out of sleep feeling battered, to the sound of Esther putting a cup of tea on the cabinet and the touch of her hand on his shoulder.

'Did you have a nice time yesterday?' she asked innocently as his eyes flashed wide open. 'You said to wake you in time for work.'

'Nice time? Work?' he said stupidly.

'Yes, you haven't woken up yet. You went out with the lads from the office yesterday. I can't remember where you said you were going. A bit of work, and then some show or other?' She gave a wicked grin and kissed him. 'I know us wives aren't supposed to ask about these things, but I hope you enjoyed it, anyway. It's nice to see you going out and enjoying yourself for a change. You work too hard.'

Kevin sat up, winced, and quickly lay down again as he realised his buttocks were sore.

She passed him his robe. 'Do you want me to turn the shower on, darling?'

'No, no,' he blurted, his mind racing. 'I can do it in a moment, after I've had my tea.'

To his relief she left him alone. He climbed out of bed and peered over his shoulder into the mirror. Thankfully the weals were almost non-existent, they just felt pronounced. The hot water of the shower burned, so he suffered under the cold for a moment. He winced as he rubbed his tender penis, but couldn't help smiling slightly in recollection. Blimey, he'd lost another whole day. How did that woman manage it?

At lunchtime he went out and bought Esther a bottle of perfume. It wasn't guilt, he told himself. Not at all. He just wanted to buy his wife a present.

He knew he'd have to get her pregnant pretty soon; give her something to keep her happy. Then all of a sudden he remembered how sexy she had been on Saturday night, how the men had all fancied her, how they had been invited to the Mansell's next party. He recalled it with a rush of possessive pride. And he remembered the sex afterwards. The unexpectedly rampant sex against the wall in the hall. Fidelity rushed over him. Dammit. Next time he was with the bitch, he'd tell her straight. He wouldn't do it again, she could go beg as much as she liked. He would stick with his wife.

On reflection, he bought Esther some earrings as well. He showed them to his mate, Charlie, at work.

'Guilty as sin,' Charlie said cheerfully. 'Never give them presents, it's a dead give-away! Go home and give her a good hot-rodding and she'll never suspect. Though if I had a wife like yours I wouldn't be bowling my balls at anybody else's wicket anyway.'

Kevin couldn't bear to waste his hard-earned money, however, and gave the presents to Esther.

'That's so clever of you!' Esther exclaimed. 'Honey, I'll wear them to the Mansell's. How did you know I was so fed up with my old ones?'

Kevin blushed guiltily.

The Mansell's party was everything Kevin thought it would be. The house was huge, and the dinner party consisted of ten couples who baited each other in the correct pecking order throughout the meal. Esther, bless her, was wearing a bright red dress made of something stretchy which, he thought, looking around the room reflectively, would have looked tacky on any other woman present. On Esther it looked a million dollars, and everyone knew it. He was feeling very protective, very aroused, and very, very confused.

Frank Brachlyn was next to her – whether by accident or design Kevin couldn't work out – and she played him like an ace. Kevin listened unashamedly as she teased, bluffed, and conned her way through all six courses without giving her hand away, and without compromising him, either. Wow, some girl, he thought proudly.

As the evening wore on the wine made him mellow, and as Esther was otherwise engaged, he made himself very pleasant to the elderly female next to him.

'You must make up the numbers in our Ascot party,' she invited him enthusiastically, not realising that he hadn't yet quite attained the inner circle. Ascot! The firm paid for it all; the train, the champagne, the tickets. Ascot! He agreed with alacrity and buttered her up some more.

The next day his boss found out that his own boss's wife had invited Kevin to Ascot, and wondered what they saw in the creep that he had missed. Kevin shortly found himself in his boss's office.

'I've been thinking about your career,' his boss boomed with jovial condescension. 'I think it's time you took up another level of responsibility, my man. Join the team, so to speak.'

'Kevin, that's wonderful!' Esther exclaimed that evening. She threw her arms around his neck and kissed him. 'I'm so proud of you!'

The next day when he went home he found she'd bought a bottle of wine for them to celebrate with. He'd never seen her like this. She sparkled. She took his shoes off and kissed his toes, which unexpectedly sent immediate signals to other regions. Bloody hell, he thought, looking down at her short curls. He rather liked her new haircut now he'd got used to it.

Then she smiled up at him with innocent trust before slowly and sensuously removing everything else he was wearing, and giving him the best massage he'd had in a long time. On the rug in the living room. He lay there enjoying this unexpected treat, and thanking the stars that his skin had reverted to its normal hue.

'Kevin?'

'Yes?' He was wallowing in the feel of her hands teasing his tense shoulders, and didn't look up.

'Can I ask you something?'

'What, honey?'

'Do you fancy me?'

He was shocked. He rolled over. 'Fancy you? What on earth do you mean? You're my wife.'

'I mean,' she hung her head, 'do you still want me as a woman. Not just a wife.'

He stared up at her. 'God, honey,' he said, realising it

was true, 'right now I could fuck the pants off you.'

She blushed prettily.

'Oh, perhaps I shouldn't have said that,' he apologised. 'It was crude.'

'It's okay,' she soothed. 'That's what I wanted to know. I was afraid...'

He gave her a big hug. 'I love you all ways, honey. In bed you're wonderful, and out of bed you're terrific.' He saw a look of miserable indecision forming. 'Come on, out with it honey. If there's something bothering you, tell me. After all this time we have no secrets, have we?'

'Well,' she went on, 'I do have this fantasy... You're not going to hate me, are you?'

'Of course not. What fantasy?'

'Sort of... oh,' she flushed to the roots of her hair. 'I have this fantasy that a man comes in during the day, and rapes me.'

'Hurts you?'

'Not hurt, rape, you idiot,' she said, somewhat more sharply than she intended.

'But that's the same thing, isn't it?' He was confused.

'Of course it isn't. Fantasy rape is about being desirable, attractive, wanted so badly that a man can't help himself; when some attractive hulk comes in and seduces you with serious intent. You're forced, but inside it's Okay. because the person who's doing it is sympathetic and wants you because you're wonderful, not because you're female and available. That's what makes it different from real rape.'

'What are you saying, honey?'

She hung her head even more, and whispered. 'I'd like you to make my fantasy come true.'

'What?' he gasped. 'You want me to rape you?'

'Yes, well, play-act it. You know.'

He really was taken aback. 'Damn it, it's a bit... I don't know whether...'

'Oh, it doesn't matter. Forget I ever said anything.'

'No, honey.' He raised himself on one elbow and fished harder for understanding. 'You mean, you want me to come in here pretending to be someone else and – and force myself on you?'

Esther nodded. 'Yes,' she said meekly, 'that's about it.'

'Why?' he asked, somewhat indignantly. 'Isn't it good enough straight?'

'Yes, but...'

He was hurt and confused. 'But, what?'

'Oh, I don't know.'

Then her hands were on him, and he couldn't think of anything else but the need to make love to this strange wife of his.

The next day at work he asked Charlie, 'Does your wife ever have fantasies?'

Charlie laughed. 'All the bloody time, mate!'

'I mean, sexual fantasies.'

'What other kind is there?'

'And that's all right with you?'

'Tell you what. If you're bothered, tell me what the fantasy is,' he winked, 'and I'll go see to it for you. Then you can do my missus some time.'

Kevin nearly hit him – then he began to think. Perhaps it wasn't so wrong for her to have fantasies; he sure as hell did – and then some. He just hadn't expected it, that was all.

But what should he do? Should he just go in and pounce one day, her knowing it was him? Would she pretend she didn't know, or should he wear a hood? How in heaven's name did you play a game like that?

Yet, despite his uncertainty, the more he thought about it the more he liked the idea. Creeping into the house, tying her up, maybe. Should he do that? Yeah, probably. However, the thought of her knowing it was him spoiled it. He just couldn't bear the thought of it all going wrong, and for her to reject him because the fantasy had not been the experience she anticipated.

His brow furrowed in thought.

Perhaps it would be better if it wasn't quite what she expected. Not hurt her, exactly, but put her off from thinking things like that again before the silly girl ended up getting hurt for real.

He began to think of some of the things the dominatrix had done to him. He wondered about gags; she'd probably scream otherwise. He wondered about restraints; were they necessary? He'd had all sorts of leather gismos used on him – not counting the whip. But then, she was a woman; he was, perforce, stronger. A woman would have to think about how to quickly restrain a man to make him less of a threat. To a man, a woman was not a threat, really. He could overpower her without tying her down at all.

Recalling the delicious sense of vulnerability he'd felt at the mysterious woman's hands, however, he decided restraints were an important part of the whole thing – definitely necessary. Almost subconsciously he began to plan, and as he planned he got more interested in the idea.

Just thinking about it turned him on something rotten.

'If you really were going to do a fantasy thing on your wife, what would you do?' he eventually asked Charlie.

His mate grinned. 'Who said anything about "if"? The unexpected always works best, I've discovered. Lull them into complacency, let them stew, let them get over the idea, then pounce – you know!'

Kevin blushed, suddenly feeling inadequate. 'No, I really don't know. I'm not very good at this kind of thing – at least, I don't think I am,' he added doubtfully.

'Well, that's a bloody first,' Charlie said cheerfully. 'Never thought I'd hear Kev the stud say he wasn't good at something.' Charlie was immediately more helpful. 'Now what she'd be thinking is milkman, postman, or some passing stranger to just come in and do her in her own home, see?'

'Really?' Kevin said doubtfully.

'Well, you have to be more clever than that. Home is too easy, too safe. You have to get her somewhere else. That would be the real thrill.'

'Do I?' Kevin wasn't convinced. 'Like where?'

Charlie shrugged. 'Use your imagination. In a wood. In a hotel. To work, it has to be unexpected. She's probably thought of more in-house scenarios than you could in a year: the dustman and the window-cleaner variety, but I bet her horizons haven't broadened past those boundaries yet.'

Kevin was taken aback by Charlie's confident assessing of his wife's fantasising. And he was a bit taken-aback that Charlie was treating it all as though it was so normal. Was it so normal? Was he just being naïve?

'But what if I do it so well that she screams, not realising it's me?' he said eventually.

Charlie chuckled. 'Then you'll probably have the police hauling your arse into a station before your feet touch.

'You have to plan it right. You have to get in there, grab her, and get her immobilised. Then she isn't sure, see? She has to wonder whether it really is you or not for it to work right. But that's what it's all about. That's part of the fun. She wants to be overpowered.'

Kevin was reluctant to do it, he realised. Not because he was afraid to play games – secretly he rather like the idea – but because he was afraid of losing her. What if he really scared her? What if she said stuff about fantasies but couldn't hack it real time? He might disgust her so much he'd lose her. But then, he thought, if she wasn't scared, where was the thrill? And it was her who had asked, so surely she'd thought about the consequences? His mind was working overtime on the project, and the more he thought, the more he realised he couldn't simply let it drop. It was becoming a driving need in him; the thought of giving his own wife a surprise party was eating at him like a canker, taking precedence over any thoughts of any of the bimbos he had vaguely been thinking of seducing.

Esther very reluctantly decided her ploy of open invitation hadn't worked. Kevin was, if anything, more complacent than usual. It had been almost a week now, and he'd not made any moves whatsoever, not even the usual bonk in the dark. He was even suspiciously ebullient, and it occurred to her that perhaps he had a mistress somewhere

– not just his usual casual bonk, but a mistress. Her eyes narrowed at the thought. It was clearly time to give him another thrashing – to get him back in the way of things.

All he could talk about was his business successes. His sudden rise within the hierarchy at the bank, the newly-opened horizons, business lunches, cosy evening get-togethers, nights at the opera, all expenses paid. Except that they weren't cosy, not to Esther. They were hard work all the way; chatting up wrinkled men who just wanted to get their hands in her knickers, sucking up to their equally wrinkled and painted wives.

And now another dinner loomed.

'Better buy a new dress, honey,' Kevin said unexpectedly. 'But be careful parking – there's been a spate of car thefts recently. You know, I'd be much happier if you parked in the multi-storey on the edge of town. Better get there early, too, if you don't want any hassle. You'll be able to do your shopping and get out before the lunch hour rush.'

'Oh, stop fussing,' she told him, pecking his cheek. But the seeds of doubt had been sown. There had been thefts from the town centre car-park, he was right. And it was annoying if you couldn't park easily, so she took his advice and got there nice and early, cruising upward until she found a nice wide place to park in. She was happy about getting out, but lack of practice driving made her a bit scared of damaging someone else's car when squeezing into the narrow spaces allocated in car parks.

Smiling happily, she went shopping. She settled on a long dress, very severe at the front, but with a low back and a slit up one side almost to her panties. That should cause a stir. She was still happy about her choice when she got back to her car to find it almost hemmed in by a largish van. She frowned, not sure she would even be able to open the driver's door of her car to slide in.

She pressed the remote to unlock her car, only realising she was not alone when a figure appeared from behind the van and grabbed her. She caught a brief glimpse of a boiler-suited figure wearing a woollen hood, then her arms were trapped to her sides and a hand clamped over her mouth, smothering her feeble attempts to scream for help.

He was very efficient. With no fuss at all he hauled her into the back of the van and pulled the door closed. Suddenly she was on her back, staring up at her faceless captor as he knelt astride her, knees on her arms. She gasped and tried to scream again, but something cold and wet was thrust into her mouth, which was then sealed in with a strip of plaster or sticky tape, she couldn't see which.

This was real and she was so afraid she almost wet herself. She whimpered with fear and struggled, realising for the first time ever just how inadequate she was in the muscle department.

'Quiet!' Her captor hissed violently. 'I won't hurt you if you do as you're told. Now, shut up!'

She whimpered again and tried to control her fear. This couldn't be happening. Not in a public car park! What did he want with her? She had no money, it couldn't be that...

Her captor shuffled down slightly and roughly tugged the hem of her T-shirt from her trousers. Oh, no, now she realised. He rucked her T-shirt up over her bra and she heard him gasp at the first sight of her white flesh. Then he lifted one knee slightly and released an arm. She immediately tried to hit him, and scrabbled at the tape on her mouth, but he merely held her wrist, reached underneath and undid her bra clip. Her furious struggles just made it all the easier for him to then slip her arm from her garments. He then stretched her arm out to the side and buckled something securely around her wrist. The clothes were then pulled up over her head, her left arm released long enough for her to be stripped to the waist, and then that arm, too, was pinioned to the other side of the van.

Her breath now was coming in ragged whimpers.

'Don't panic,' her captor was whispering. 'I'm not going to hurt you. Listen! I have no intention of hurting you. Just relax, accept it, and you'll end up totally unharmed. We're just going to have a bit of fun, that's all.'

An inexplicable urge to laugh rose in her throat. Only last week she'd begged Kevin to let her live out a fantasy, and here it was happening. Only it wasn't Kevin, it was some stranger and it wasn't a fantasy. There was nothing she could do with her arms spread invitingly, and her firm breasts rising towards this monster as she breathed deeply to quell her panic. Her hands clutched helplessly at thin air out of harm's way, and she made begging noises in her throat.

A finger brushed across her breasts and down to her navel. She shuddered involuntarily. 'Not yet, little lady,' he whispered, guessing she was begging to be released. 'We're going to spend some time getting acquainted, having a good time, then I'll let you go. You'll like this, believe me, and no one but you will be any the wiser afterwards. Now let's see what else you have to offer me, eh?'

She glared at him furiously, now believing that he wasn't going to strangle her or cut her into ribbons, and her noises turned to those of helpless anger. To her horror he slipped down the zip of her jeans, flipped open the button, and pulled them down a few inches. She heard him gasp again and realised he was already rampant with desire.

'My, you're a little beauty,' he wheezed. 'We're going to enjoy this, oh yes!'

She heard people outside the van and began to wriggle violently and whimper into the gag. Her captor suddenly burst into life, reached over to the cab and turned on the radio, drowning any other noises which might have attracted attention.

With her legs momentarily freed she lifted a knee with all her force and tried to catch him in the groin, but he anticipated the move and avoided the catastrophe.

'You little vixen,' he admonished. 'Trying to sabotage my tool-kit before I get to show you the plumbing?'

She growled with frustration.

'Tell you what,' he went on, 'we need to find some more secluded surroundings. Let's go for a little ride.' While he spoke he ignored her pleas and stretched her ankles towards the back corners of the van and tied them there.

Esther wriggled, testing the straps, only to find that they were firm. She began to feel a faint moistening between her legs at the exposed position, even though she still had her jeans on.

Her captor slid a hand down her flattened tummy, tucked his fingers beneath the zip of her jeans, and pressed a finger against the moist crevice discovered there. 'Goodness,' he said, clearly amused. 'I do believe you're enjoying this. Let's give you something to think about while we're driving, shall we?'

She didn't like the sound of that, and shook her head violently, but he took no notice. She squealed with horror as he pulled her jeans down over her buttocks, which was as far as they would go with her legs stretched wide, and that gave her a small moment of satisfaction. But her complacency died instantly as he picked up a large spanner and showed it to her. 'Told you I was good with the plumbing,' he said, and inserted it in an upright position between her legs. The taut jeans held it firmly in place. She gasped at the sudden shock of cold metal against her sensitive skin, but no amount of wriggling would displace it.

'There,' he said with satisfaction. 'Now, just one more little refinement, and off we go.'

She fought with fury as he dangled a rather efficient-looking blindfold before her, but no amount of head shaking was going to stop him, and it was quickly strapped tightly over her eyes. Esther moaned abjectly, further panicked by the lack of sight. What was he doing now?

She sensed him climb over into the driver's seat, felt the van growl into life, and then they were moving. Down the ramps, round and round until they arrived at the pay booth. She held her breath as her captor cheerfully paid his fee, but made no attempt to gain the park attendant's attention. Not that she probably would have succeeded against the volume of the radio. Christ, she thought as the window rose to shut out all outside noise.

Then there was just the feel of rough fabric beneath her bare backside, the lurches and bumps of the noisy vehicle, the radio and out of tune whistling of her unknown captor, and the strange sensation of cold steel vibrating between her thighs.

She pulled continually at the cuffs that held her stretched to this stranger's bidding, and wondered where they were going. She also wondered who he was, and whether he did this sort of thing often. Obviously he had now removed the mask. It would have been nice to see quite who had kidnapped her. It was his gall that was the most disconcerting thing, though. He had taken her so easily, so efficiently, and in broad daylight. And no one would even know she was missing. Not for hours and hours.

All sorts of things went through her mind, but nothing could block out the sexual awareness of her own naked breasts bouncing to the heavy suspension of the van, and the incongruous use of the spanner nestling between her legs.

'Enjoying yourself, darling?' The driver was shouting over the noise of the radio, and she detected a faint accent. North country, perhaps.

She growled and yanked at the straps.

They seemed to be driving for an awfully long time, and over some very bumpy roads. Where the hell were they? They had to be miles and miles away from the city by now.

Then the road seemed to get bumpier and bumpier. The van finally pulled to a halt and the engine was cut. So was the radio. Esther froze. She heard the front door open, then to her horror the back doors opened too, letting in a cool breeze and the sound of birdsong.

She felt the back of the van dip as he climbed up. 'Oh, what a nice view,' he whispered coarsely; she gathered he wasn't talking of the countryside, which she could smell.

She felt his knees between her legs and his hands rest on her body, then he leaned forward and the softest touch of a tongue rasped over her right nipple. He leaned against the spanner, embedded tight between her thighs. She inhaled sharply as a wave of primitive sexual awareness drove goosebumps up all over her body. He wheezed as he licked his way all over her breasts, down to her waist, his tongue rasping against her flesh like that of a cat. And all the while the metal spanner was rubbing erotically against the small nub of roused flesh.

Her fears were swept away by urges so primitive they shocked the tiny core of her awareness, and any tiny niggling hope that it was Kevin fled. He would never in a hundred years have done anything like this. As the licking continued she found her body traitorously responding, writhing beneath the animal who slobbered over her.

'Like that, bitch?' he croaked between licks, then worked his way back up to her breasts, and rolled her nipples with his tongue until she was shuddering with every movement. She felt pressure building inside her until she wanted to scream – and then suddenly he was gone. She was lying alone, a summer breeze cooling her flushed flesh with a feather-light touch.

She sensed he was watching, and tried to lie still, but could not stop the betraying ripples which pulsed through her muscles. Then he climbed out of the van. He released her ankles and ripped the jeans away hastily. Now she was totally naked. Exposed. Out in the country, tied up in the back of a van. Reality intruded: anyone could look in!

She tried to clamp her legs shut, to hide herself, but he pushed them determinedly apart and once more encased her ankles in straps. She moaned and moved, feeling the breeze against the moist orifice which was opened invitingly to her captor.

She heard his breath quicken as he pushed her ankles, bent her knees, and attached the cuffs somewhere over her head, to the ceiling of the van. She squealed with annoyance and pulled. She bounced on the end of some kind of elastic. There was a slight give, and then the elastic rebounded with an undignified lurch.

She tensed. Now he would have his lecherous way with her.

But no. She gasped as something cold dripped between her legs. He smoothed it in. Then he began to massage her. Softly and firmly, his strong hands massaged the whole area until she was totally oiled. She tried to move away from his hands, but found herself in the embarrassing position of total subjugation. And she could not just relax and compliantly accept the treatment. The sensations were too overpowering, too glorious to tolerate in acquiescence. Her mind might rebel, but her treacherous body was revelling in the novel experience. So her knees bent and straightened with his ministrations, giving every indication of enjoyment to her tormentor, who by now was making some very interesting moaning noises himself.

His fingers were gradually getting more intimate, sliding in and out of her vagina, wetting the lips, spreading the oil within. She gave a muffled scream when his finger slipped into her anus, but could do nothing but lie there and accept as it happened again and again. Oh, no one had ever done that to her before; saving her vibrator in the darkness of the night it was virgin territory.

'Like that, do you, princess?' he whispered.

She moaned and her head rolled from side to side.

Then he leaned forward, arms around her legs, his chest pressing her thighs against her breasts. As he began to kiss her throat she realised he had removed his clothes, and was rampant as the tip of his penis teased at her moist sex lips.

She moaned.

'Tell me to do it,' he whispered softly. 'I won't until you beg me.'

Conceited arsehole! Beg? Esther would never do that! But the dark stimulation had dragged her into another world, a previously unknown world where nothing existed other than the sensations of her own body. Was this how it had been for Kevin?

The man thrust again and again at her vagina and anus – just a little pressure, a little stretching, sliding, then away. She moaned with desire, with need, with shock at her own wish for him to continue. The frustration was awful. She began to rise to meet his every thrust, but he pulled away each time. God, the man was inhuman!

'Beg me,' he whispered in a husky voice. 'Not until you beg me. You know you want to. Just nod, and I'll slide in and fuck you – like you want me to.'

Her useless hands clasped and unclasped, and she thrashed in the dilemma of desire against conscience. But in the anonymity of darkness, need won. Eventually, battling with a turmoil of conflicting emotions, she breathed deeply and gave the faintest of nods.

The brute saw this.

Again there was a faint pressure against the entrance of her vagina, then a further widening as he sank what felt like an enormous erection inside her. Slick and ready, she felt him glide in right to the hilt until his balls rubbing softly against her stimulated bottom. She moaned with pleasure.

Then he moved back. She gasped with regret as she felt him begin to slide away. She wanted to say it was all right, she didn't hurt, please go on! Her breath was ragged and she could feel the onset of orgasm shooting up through her middle as he exited totally, then, before she could grunt her displeasure, he began again. Never had anything prepared her for the sheer erotic joy of this slow and controlled sex.

It was everything she had hoped for. And the fact that she could do nothing to stop it was the most stimulating thing she had ever experienced. Eventually this slow, grinding pressure became too much for her, and she gave a small muffled noise as the force of her orgasm broke through her body. As he felt it, her captor gave a groan, a few sharp thrusts, and came too. They both panted for a moment, then her captor slid out and moved away, leaving her cold and alone.

Finally he unclipped her ankles, and as she lay in the darkness, she knew her fantasy had finally been realised. She had enjoyed sex with a completed stranger. Not only that, but she had begged him for it.

With the gradual retreat of her sexual high, she once again became aware that she was lying trussed and naked in the back of a van, doors open to the outside.

'Want some more, darling?' he drawled.

She shook her head wearily.

'Well you'll have to wait a bit. I'm just going to have a bite of lunch while I recover, then I might oblige you. It's an absolutely beautiful day, you know.'

She pulled at the restraints around her wrists.

'You promise not to start yelling – not that there's anyone to hear you – and I'll take out the gag and give you a beer. Yes?'

She stopped fidgeting and nodded reluctantly.

'I'll take that as an affirmative, and don't forget, it won't take me a second to stuff it back in, okay?'

Before he took out the gag, however, he tied her ankles firmly together, released her other bonds, tied her hands behind her back, and pulled her out of the van. 'A breath of fresh air wouldn't do you any harm, I guess,' he said.

She grunted as his shoulder sank into her middle and he lifted, and she realised he had dressed again. Then she was dumped on the grass, naked and bound.

'Now, you just kneel there and let me get you all comfy.'

She found herself kneeling upright with her shoulders pressed to the horizontal limb of a tree. He threaded a rope under her arms and over her breasts and tied her tightly, then untied her arms and spread them along the limb, securing them firmly to its length. Then, very carefully, he picked the sticky tape from her mouth and pulled out the packing. 'Now don't you go getting noisy on me,' he threatened, holding a can to her lips.

When she had gulped the precious liquid, she said, 'Can I ask you a question?'

'Yep. I might not answer, though.'

'Why me?'

'Because I've been watching you and I just couldn't resist your so very blatant charms, darling. I just knew you'd be a sexual animal if I got you away from the veneer of civilisation.'

She wasn't sure if that was a compliment or not. 'Do I know you?' she asked tentatively.

He chuckled. 'Now, that would be telling.'

'Do you know me?' she persisted.

'I'm getting to know you.'

She was silent for a moment, and heard him moving about. 'Are you going to hurt me?' she asked, not really wanting to know the answer.

'Have I hurt you yet?'

'No...'

'In fact, I'd say you've enjoyed it so far.'

'Maybe,' she said, not wanting to admit that to herself, let alone him, 'but...'

'You either have or you haven't.'

She couldn't answer that. 'Please untie me,' she said instead. 'Enough is enough.'

She felt hands at her ankles, and gave a sigh of relief which turned into a wail as he pulled them apart and tied them to something rough. A fallen branch? Now she was kneeling with her arms stretched out and her knees apart, once again, totally vulnerable and available. 'You can't have enough of a good thing,' he sniggered.

'I don't...' she began.

'That's enough! One more word and in goes the gag.'

She sensed he meant it and shut up instantly.

He knelt behind her and fondled her while he drank his beer, feeding both his appetites at the same time. Then he pushed a thin branch down between her legs and into the ground behind her. It flexed upward, and with every tiny, involuntary movement she inadvertently rubbed herself on it. The strange vulnerability of her position and her inability to stop this stimulation made her juices flow.

'That's how the native women do it,' he informed her.

'Do what?'

'Bring themselves off,' he said crudely. 'I read it in a book.'

He then poured beer on her breasts and sucked it off, poured beer on her tongue and tasted it, and all the time she was moving against the foreign object between her legs, only now her movements weren't quite so involuntary. She was doing it because it was good.

He stood back after a while and watched as she stimulated herself almost to orgasm. She was gasping with need, the thin veneer of sophistication totally erased. There was nothing outside this wonderful bondage and the exhilarating sexual freedom it gave her. She was not in control of her own body, and so could have no fear of her responses.

She heard movement, and the branch dipped. She felt the harsh rasp of his zipper against her cheek, and then the warm pulsing hardness of his cock against her chin. She felt beer dripping to her lips, and on to his cock. She tasted it, reached for it. She began to suck. She sucked the beer from his tight balls, and nibbled and tasted her way upward until the back of her head was jammed against the branch, immobilised. She felt him press towards her, his hands pulling on the branch, effectively guiding her head back and forth.

She reached for the tip, sucked, rubbed her tongue around the beer-washed penis, and took it in her mouth. He groaned. She sucked harder, and he began to lean forward, gripping the branch while her seeking mouth pleasured him, her mind filled with wonder that she was doing this thing because she wanted to. The twig moved up and down her lower body as he pulled her about, but not enough. She groaned with frustration, with need, used her tongue, sucked and teased to encourage him to push at the branch to which she was strung. Harder and harder he pulled until he was ramming his engorged cock into her throat, jamming her chin into the zipper of his jeans with every stroke. She felt him straining, knew he was going to come and screamed with frustration. The vibrations in her throat increased, he pushed hard and she gagged, swallowing him deep into her throat as he shot his viscous seed into her with a strangled cry of triumph.

After a couple of seconds he eased up, allowing her to gasp for breath. Then he leaned his hands on the branch, slid his limp penis from her mouth and began to move her hips for her, rubbing her against the rough branch below until her sighs became desperate gasps of need. He didn't stop until eventually she shuddered dramatically on the craggy bark, wracked with satisfaction and fulfilment.

'Oh, baby, you're something else,' her captor whispered.

Ester frowned. Surely she knew that voice. 'Who—?' she began, but the packing was suddenly thrust into her mouth. 'Nnnng!' she yelled, trying to spit it out, but it was followed by the inevitable sticky tape.

'Regrettably, princess,' he said in his strong northern accent, 'I have to get back to my job. I think I'll pick you up again some time, though. You enjoyed it too much for it not to be repeated. From now on you'll be looking over your shoulder for me. You'll be waiting with anticipation, but you won't know when I'll come, and you won't know when you're walking near me in the street. But I'll know you. Oh, baby, I'll remember you all right.'

Esther could not say all the rude things she wanted to say, and was bundled into the back of the van and roughly but efficiently put back into her bra and T-shirt. When she tried to lift her hands to her face to rip away the sticky tape he slapped them down hard.

'Do that, darling, and I'll dump you out of the van without your clothes,' he warned. She gave in, knowing that anyone prepared to kidnap her would not be afraid to carry out such a threat. When her top half was clothed he tied her arms behind her back, before pulling her jeans up and fastening them. Then he crossed her ankles, tied them, and roped them to her wrists behind her back, effectively hog-tying her.

'You sexy little whore,' he said, before climbing out and slamming the rear door.

In spite of everything that had happened, Esther found the constriction of her present situation as satisfying as all the rest, and wallowed in weary pleasure.

The man didn't speak to her again.

She only realised she was back at her car when the door was opened, the rope on her hands was cut, and she was dragged and dumped on a seat. By the time she'd freed her eyes to discover she was in her own car the van was just a couple of red lights disappearing down the exit ramp. And by the time she'd removed the gag and managed to untie her feet, she knew he would be long gone. There was no point racing after him.

Her first thought was to call the police. But what would she tell them? She hadn't been harmed and she had no evidence that she'd been abducted.

Besides, she thought with a sly grin, she knew deep down it was Kevin – his corny northern accent gave him away. And the dear love had certainly fulfilled her fantasy and made her year – let alone her day!

Chapter Eleven

Madam Tisset was not amused by Esther's adventure in the country, because she couldn't comprehend that her most promising pupil had actually enjoyed the experience.

'My dear girl,' she said grimly, 'I think the time has come for you to have another learning experience. I have a gentleman for you to dominate thoroughly today. He's a civil servant – he thinks I don't know that – and he needs a really painful session to keep him on his toes at work.'

She led Esther through to where a tall thin man sat, knees together primly. 'Get up,' Madam Tisset snapped, jolting him out of a daydream. Whatever it was about he'd been enjoying it, judging by the rather obvious bulge in his trousers.

'Sorry, Madam Tisset,' he stuttered nervously, his pale eyes watering slightly. 'I didn't hear you come in.'

'You will be sorry,' she said grimly. 'Now, say hello to your dominatrix for today. She's my latest pupil, and she'll be taking this session.'

Esther almost felt sorry for the puny man. She felt an immediate sense of power, and gave a dazzling smile as her eyes raked him. 'Scared?' she said scornfully.

The taunt worked. He pulled in his belly and puffed out an inadequate chest, and spoke directly to Madam Tisset, ignoring Esther with all the disdain he could muster. 'I'll try her out, Madam Tisset, but I warn you, if the session is not good, you'll get no fee.'

'You can give him twenty extra lashes for that,' she retorted instantly, turning to Esther. 'On his dick, if you can find it. He should know better than to threaten me.'

'Oh, I'll find it,' Esther said, in a tone filled with husky promise. 'In what way do you suggest I punish the subject?'

'The little tart likes to dress as a woman, don't you, whore?'

'Yes, Madam Tisset,' the man said, his eyes beginning to darken at the mere sound of her vitriolic scorn.

'And then he likes me to fish beneath his skirt and pull out the offending article, and punish it for being there, doesn't he?'

'Yes, Madam Tisset,' he gasped.

'The little boy thinks it's a dirty object which really should be there, doesn't he? So I have to try to pull it out at the roots, and it's really got to hurt the dirty little boy, hasn't it?' She walked up close to him and was breathing into his face, her lips curled back into a snarl of disgust.

Now he didn't answer, but was staring at her, almost panting with anticipation.

'Go and wash,' she snapped, turning away. 'And use the scrubbing brush really hard. I'll be watching.'

He obediently trotted out of the room, and Madam Tisset's severe demeanour slipped instantly. 'Would you like a cup of tea, my dear, while he gets himself psyched up, or would you like something stronger?'

'A glass of wine would go down well,' Esther said, knowing her cupboard was well stocked.

'Help yourself, my dear. Now, you really mustn't be

apprehensive. He's the same as all the other inadequate little men I get in here. Whatever authority he thinks he has comes off with his clothes. Don't you worry about hurting him, you just worry about not pleasing him, because I don't want to have to sue him for my money.'

Esther looked shocked. 'You wouldn't?'

'Damn right I would, and he knows it. I've got him by the short and curlies. At least, I would have if I wasn't honest. That's why he keeps coming back to me; he trusts me. So do all my clients. It's the single most important thing next to being good at what you do. They have to feel safe when they're back outside in the big bad world. They have to believe in your professional discretion. That's why I don't have any trouble getting my money out of them. They want to come back for more. They know, more than anyone, what a useful job we do. It's a bit like the coalition, my dear, which was an institution run by a few old men afraid of enjoying themselves. If the ban on prostitution was lifted everyone would be a damn sight happier.' She slumped onto a chair, slipped off a shoe and rubbed her foot. 'Oh my, these shoes will be the death of me. Now, get out of your togs.'

'What should I wear?' Esther asked.

'You can keep your clothes on if you want, but you might get rather warm. He likes to be hooded, and judging from the hard-on he gets, he's got a good imagination. He gets quite a pressure build up, does this one. Surprising, really, he doesn't look capable of it. But then, things are seldom what they seem at first glance.

'Now, you go to the dungeon, get ready, and I'll bring him to you.'

From the dungeon, a dark room lit by flickering candle-bulbs, Esther heard Madam Tisset giving orders.

'Harder, you disgusting little slut, scrub harder! Let's see it really glow. That's much better. Now get your frock on – parading it about like that as if you're proud of it, you perverted worm. Now shut your eyes, how dare you look at your betters? Now run your hands down the frock, make sure it's nice and tidy. All over, that's right, and again, see if you can flatten it a bit more down the front... Now, put this collar on, you filthy beast. From this moment on you're a prisoner of the Turks, and you know what they do to little boys, don't you? They take their balls and squeeze them in a vice until they go black and drop off. Then they can sing like canaries and pee like little girls. That's what you really want, isn't it? Come along, my associate is waiting for you.'

Madam Tisset walked in leading the man by a chain. He wore a short white dress. It pinched his waist in, pushing his chest and bottom out. The gathered but very short skirt lifted out over a pair of white hairless legs. He had his eyes tight shut as ordered, which was just as well, because it was all Esther could do not to giggle. But a warning glance from her tutor made her concentrate.

'Now,' Madam Tisset said to her, 'a nice thick belt, please, the one with wrist restraints at the back. That's right. Now, breathe in hard, slut, your waist isn't quite as small as it should be. You haven't been doing your exercises, now have you?'

She cinched the belt in hard until he winced, then buckled his wrists into the small of his back. Then standing back slightly, she lifted the hem of his skirt and showed

Esther that he certainly had an erection.

Then she handed her the lead. 'He's all yours. Deal harshly with him, he deserves it.' She winked, pointed to a leather hood hanging on a hook, and left.

For a moment Esther was at a loss, but then her hands reached out for the hood almost of their own accord. 'Kneel down, slut,' she said as harshly as she could. 'I have to hood you so you don't look at that revolting penis of yours.'

She pulled the hood over his head and buckled it onto him. It was probably his own, she thought, judging from the perfect fit, and seeing how the leather straps were marked in all the right places as she pulled the fastenings tight.

'Now, open your mouth.'

To Esther's surprise, her voice had almost instantly attained a quality of command Madam Tisset herself would have been proud of, and her final feelings of unease fled as she squeezed a large ball gag into the man's mouth. 'Suck on that,' she ordered, buckling the gag tightly around his face, pulling his cheeks back into a fixed smile. He gave a gurgle of complaint.

'What? Do you want me to take it back out? Do you want me to hand you your clothes and send you away from here right now? No? Then thank me, you ungrateful slut, and spread your legs!'

'Nnnng,' he groaned, quivering with anticipation.

After a moment her subject was standing to attention, his hands buckled firmly behind his back, his legs parted with a spreader. A chain from the ceiling fixed to his gag kept him immobile, and his thin dick was dripping like a leaky tap.

'Now you're mine, you dirty little whore,' Esther whispered. 'Now I can do what I want with you, and there's nothing you can do to stop me.' As her hand slid up the inside of his thigh he jerked, vibrant with expectation, and his dick pulsed just once, then his whole body tensed, quivering.

She ran her hand up his other thigh, squeezed his balls tight, and twisted. He jerked again, making low growling noises in his throat. Recalling what Madam Tisset had said about pulling it out at the roots, she realised that this man liked to be punished. Armed with this knowledge, she bound his balls up tightly in a complicated mesh of straps designed for the purpose.

He was moving slightly, his hips grinding from left to right, and she realised he was gone, descended into his own private world, and that she did not need to speak any more.

Taking a thin cane from the wall she ran it softly up and down his legs, lifting the skirt and letting it fall again. Then she drew her hand back and slashed the cane down. The sound of it on naked skin far exceeded the force with which it was propelled, and he jumped, for the first thing he knew about the target was the sting of the cane's arrival.

Satisfied that this was what he wanted, Esther drew her arm back and chose a new target. After a while she fell into the swing of it. Instead of wondering whether the man was enjoying himself – though she had no doubt that he was – she began to warm to the action, choosing her targets carefully to avoid the growing criss-cross of lines up and down his legs, and finding virgin skin to mark as her own.

Once she had claimed almost every inch of bare flesh on his legs, she moved in to smooth her hands over the ridges, to feel the tiny raised weals he now wore on his legs up to the hem of his skirt. She rubbed up under his skirt and felt tantalising fresh ground beneath it. Quivering with a strange pleasure, she lifted the skirt and tucked it into the belt around his waist, digging her fingers hard into his already constricted middle.

Now his excitement became increasingly evident in the urgent thrusting of his hips and the rampant erection that thrust from the confines of the cock straps.

She gently tapped the erection with the cane and saw it bounce upward eagerly. Gosh, Madam Tisset really did mean she should hit him there! Tentatively at first, then with increasing skill, she began to target the long finger of veined skin. The noises the man was making were a mixture of strangled grunts and gasps, and she was sure his cries of anguish were the result of hanging on to his control for as long as he possibly could.

Eventually, though, his willpower began to wilt under the wicked onslaught. On a normal part of his body the cane would have stung, but on his engorged penis it must have seemed vastly more destructive. As she watched, entranced, he rose upward onto the balls of his feet, looking as if he was going to explode with the effort. And explode he did. Esther was standing to one side, but almost with vindictive and subconscious knowledge he seemed to sense her position, and turned towards her as his spunk erupted from his turgid cock.

Esther looked at the mess trickling down her belly and

frowned, and at that moment Madam Tisset opened the door and came in. 'I heard you finish him off,' she said, going to the wall and taking something down.

'Should I let him go now?' Esther asked.

'Oh, no. Now he needs to do penance.' She hooked what seemed like a vast weight to the cock strap, and let go. The bound man gave a groan as it settled, taking his balls several more inches towards his knees. Then she led Esther from the room.

'There, now we leave him to enjoy his self-castigation for a bit,' she said, 'and you can go and have a shower. He always does that, you know,' she added, nodding to the mess on Esther's front. 'With unerring accuracy.'

'Does he aim for us on purpose?'

'Oh yes. You see he hates women, really. What you have to learn, my dear, is that some men have had a very strange upbringing. Women, too, of course. I see that as part of my role in life; to help them cope with their guilt, or whatever is lying inside their heads.'

'I see,' Esther said doubtfully, wondering if her husband's enjoyment of being tied up and beaten was indicative of some kind of strange complex, or more to the point, if hers was. On reflection though, she doubted it.

'But they're not all like that one, of course,' Madam Tisset carried on, settling on her settee with a sigh, and picking up a half-drunk glass of wine. 'Some of them just really like sex, and that's all part of the same game.

'Now, did you get randy doing that?' A single glance at Esther's flushed face told her the truth. 'Then you'd better bring yourself off, there's a good girl. Never leave yourself all wound up unless you've got somewhere to take it.'

Esther wiped the come off her belly with a tissue, strangely turned on by the smell of the man and her recent exertions on his body parts. It was also exciting having left him tied up in there with a weight on his balls. She realised Madam Tisset was watching her with an eager look on her face, and flushed slightly with sudden realisation. Not only did she want to do what her mentor had suggested, she wanted her to watch.

Madam Tisset sipped her wine as Esther sat opposite her on a high-backed chair, and opened her legs. Esther leaned her head back and began to pleasure herself, pushing her breasts high, then sliding her hands from breast to thigh and back up again to take her nipples between finger and thumb.

She began to move to the tune of her body, her hands slipping slightly lower with every sensuous stroke until they slid to the soft flesh between her legs, and parted the lips slowly.

Her mouth opened slightly and she began to gasp as her fingers worked their magic. It was so decadent, so exciting being watched as she masturbated. No one had ever watched her before. It really was the most shamefully erotic sensation.

She thought about the man standing in the little room with his balls sinking lower to the tune of a large weight, and his silent pain stimulated her to a point from which she could no longer hold back. Her fingers worked furiously, rubbing up and down, finding the exact level of speed to trigger the orgasm.

Madam Tisset watched avidly, breathing deeply as

Esther's nubile body writhed, and then sighed with disappointment when the show was over.

Esther glanced at her through dreamy eyes, wondering what to make of it all. What would she expect of her now?

But Madam Tisset expected no more. She smiled softly. 'Thank you for that, my dear. Now, go and have your wash, then I think we had better release him, don't you?'

The man groaned as the weight was lifted, but the tension seemed to have gone from him totally. He was as wet a rag as Esther had ever seen, and after a shower, dressed in his respectable clothes again, she found it hard to believe he would ever have allowed anyone like her or Madam Tisset within yards of him. He looked down his nose with a supercilious expression as he counted out a wadge of notes.

'She was all right,' he said grudgingly as he left. 'I'll be back at the same time in a fortnight.'

Madam Tisset giggled. 'He will be too, on the dot. He's very punctual. His wife thinks he goes to a men's club once a fortnight, you know.'

'He's married?'

'Happily, as far as I can gather, excepting in one respect, and I manage to cover that quite adequately.'

'I never thought of people like that coming to – to prostitutes.'

She used the word reluctantly, making Madam Tisset grin with malicious amusement. 'It's the oldest profession in the world, my dear. And in spite of modern technology, is as lucrative as it ever was. Most men will visit one at some time in their lives.'

'Mine better not,' Esther said.

'Why not, my dear?'

'Oh, I don't know. I mind, that's all. At least, I used to. Now I'm not so sure. In fact, I suppose I'd rather he came to you for this, than took some little strumpet to a hotel for a weekend.'

'What's the difference?'

'Well, this is business, I suppose. And if he's going to take anyone out to a hotel to be wined and dine, it should be me.'

'Bravo!'

Later, at home, Kevin was as attentive as ever. 'I've been asked to stay on late tomorrow, love,' he said, still staring into his paper. 'It might be a good idea if I stay at a hotel, because I'll probably have a couple of drinks after the meeting.'

Esther gave him a dubious glance, which he did not see. 'I'm not doing anything, I could come with you,' she suggested.

Kevin managed a strained smile. 'Oh, honey, I wouldn't subject you to this one, it's really going to be quite a bore. It's just a group of us, you know the kind of thing, all blokes together? The talk can get a bit rowdy. And the other wives aren't expected to come to this one, so you'd be on your own a bit. I'd much rather you came, honey, but it just wouldn't be right. You do understand, don't you?'

Oh, Esther understood all right.

Chapter Twelve

Tanya was waiting for him by his car, just as she said she would. She was a small, almost Eastern-looking woman with olive skin and dark hair, but her accent was pure London.

'Are you sure your husband doesn't know where you are?' he asked, quickly scanning the exits and entrances for signs of rampaging cuckolded males.

'Oh, no, he's away on the oil fields, like I told you,' she said, flashing a knowing glance. 'He knows I go out with other men. He doesn't mind, he says it works both ways.'

'What do you mean?' He unlocked the car, and they slid in together.

'Well, he goes out with those Eastern women. There's lots of them on the game, and they know some unusual techniques. When he comes back he teaches me what he's learned, and when he's away, I practice. I thought I knew about sex, but the more I learn the more I realise I didn't have a clue. In the Eastern countries women actually get lessons in sex before they get married – and I'm not talking about reproduction or the birds and the bees routines. It's a shame it doesn't happen the same in England.

He gave a silly grin. 'So what are you going to teach me?'

She responded with a faint chuckle. 'I don't know what you like; we'll have to find out, won't we?'

In Tanya's house the Eastern influence was well and truly evident. The living room was plush with dark red and gold fabrics, and upstairs the three bedrooms were all fitted out in differing styles of outrageous eroticism. In one there were erotic hangings on all the walls, and implements of love were displayed freely. The second was totally in black, with black satin sheets and a cast iron bed, and the third was bright pink and frilly, like a whore's boudoir. Kevin immediately felt movement down below, and knew he was in for a long night.

'You're sure your husband's in the Sudan?' he murmured, brushing a hand over her dark hair.

'Quite sure,' she responded huskily, falling to her knees before him, and dropping her eyes with suitable modesty. 'Master, I am yours to use as you wish. You may use me and abuse me in whatever manner you desire, and if you wish for suggestions, I'm quite happy to oblige.'

If Kevin thought he had a hard on before, it was now like a rock. It was tempting to just thrust it at her, but he knew from experience that all things were better for the waiting. 'I'd like a drink, first,' he said, settling himself on the black satin sheets.

'What would my master wish me to prepare?'

'Whisky on the rocks. Then you can go and run me a bath, and wash me.'

'Yes, master.'

He had taken his shoes off, and was lounging comfortably when she brought him a glass on a small silver tray, and placed it by the bed, saying with deferential courtesy, 'Master, if you'd like to come to the bath, I'll shower, and come to you when I'm clean.'

Kevin sank into the foamy water and closed his eyes. Bloody hell, all his life he'd been dreaming of finding a sexual submissive, but it hadn't for a moment occurred to him it would be Tanya. He had supposed himself to be in for a night of enjoyable rumpy-pumpy, but now guessed it was to be somewhat different. It just went to show that your perceptions of a person's sexual inclinations could be vastly misjudged, there being no hint of a person's inner desires in their social behaviour.

Esther came to mind briefly. Not with any kind of feelings of guilt; he had been far too unfaithful for far too long for that. No, he thought of her with a kind of mild surprise, having recently discovered that she harboured depths he had not yet trawled.

He lay there and contemplated his impressive cock, proudly rampant through the bubbles, and hoped that Tanya was as submissive as she was making out. It would be nice to have it sucked by a connoisseur. However, he was a bit confused by Tanya. He had the strangest feeling that in spite of her submissive role, she was going to pull his strings from beginning to end; a contradiction, but one he could live with if she was everything she was presently promising to be.

Subconsciously he was listening to the shower in the next room, and imagining her slick with soap and water, her dark hair plastered down her back, her fingers caressing her dark skin as she cleaned herself everywhere.

He wondered why she hadn't wanted him to do the cleaning bit. Yes, he would have liked that.

Eventually the shower stopped, and he craned his neck to get a first exciting glimpse of her flesh as she passed the door, but was disappointed to see a flash of ankle-length dressing gown which deflated his dew-speckled images. There was something so homely about a dressing gown that his cock drooped in disappointment. Kevin's lust dissipated instantly, and he sank further into the water, simply tired. What the hell was he here for? He might as well have gone home and let Esther massage his shoulders, give her a quick bonk in the dark and allow himself to succumb to the call of heavy sleep. The more he thought about it, the more the warm water lulled him into apathy. Hell, he couldn't be bothered to play games. Was there any way he could just cry off; climb out – when he'd summoned up the energy – and go home? He sighed, knowing it just wasn't an option; the poor girl would be really disappointed in him if he didn't make an effort. Besides, what could that do to his reputation? It just didn't bear thinking about.

In the bedroom he heard her moving around, then scented the pungent smell of a new jostick and heard the low chant of something discordant and foreign playing subtly in the background.

He was mentally steeling himself for the mammoth effort when there was movement behind him. His eyes opened, then widened in shock. He straightened slightly, shooting a tidal wave of bubbles onto the green carpet. For Tanya was neither in a dressing gown, nor naked and blatantly ready for sex. Instead, she was clothed head to toe in red silk heavily embroidered with exotic flowers and birds of paradise. Her long nails were painted, her wrists and ankles heavy with ornament, and her face was covered with a veil. Nothing of her body was visible, save an inch of belly complete with a navel ornament. Her hands and feet were heavy with gold jewellery, and her vivid green eyes rimmed with kohl.

As his amazed glance travelled up and down her body, she glided in, knelt in a fluid movement, and pressed her hands together in supplication before sinking back onto her heels to wait. Kevin thought himself fairly experienced in the art of eroticism, but nothing had prepared him for the exquisite anticipation of having the flesh withheld. He sat up slowly, never taking his eyes from her, and as his imagination pictured her oiled skin beneath the silk, the smooth curves of her full breast, tiredness fled. His eyes dwelled on the small swell of her middle, the indent of her belly-button, and the crease between her legs which was obscured by swathes of fine fabric.

At that moment he felt as superior as a male could ever feel. He was of the dominant species. He was lord and master to this woman, this servant, this whore, and he would use her as he saw fit. In that instant their roles were as clearly defined as if written in stone. No words were necessary.

He stared for a long time, savouring this new sensation. It was good. It had nothing to do with holding down a wriggling female form, demanding, taking what he wanted. It had far more to do with the evolution of species, that of natural female submission to his obvious male superiority.

He became suffused with a gloriously warm feeling of benevolence. Despite his earlier misgivings, he would allow this woman to feel the strength of his body, to experience the exquisite joys of his lovemaking.

He began to move, and as he did so she anticipated his needs, and rose gracefully to her feet, holding a towel between her hands. He couldn't quite work out where it had come from, but it didn't matter. Her head was still bowed submissively, waiting.

He stepped from the bath like Adonis, like Titus, and held his arms out in the diminishing sound of sloshing water. Tanya began to dry him as he waited. She lovingly dwelled on every part of his body, rubbing with small circular movements, attaining an almost clinical desire to dry every single inch of his body. His sexual organs were accorded the same precise attention, no more, no less, which created an exquisite desire to grab her hand, to make her stop what she was doing and feel how wonderfully erect he was, feel the heat of his manhood as it rose before him. The way she ignored this part of him, gave it less than the expected attention was frustrating, but strangely exciting, as if she was saving the best till last.

When he was dry to her satisfaction, she walked backward through the door, her clasped hands and bowed head indicating how much it would please her if he followed. Not a word was spoken.

He realised that the distant music comprised female voices, and guessed accurately that they were revelling in praise of the male, and all falsely nurtured visions of equality of the sexes disappeared up his backside. Men were superior, women were there to do their bidding, and it was quite all right to punish them if they failed in their duties.

She led him not to the bedroom sleek with black satin, but to the one brightly decorated in garish colours, and towards a low trestle table, suitably styled for the male body, upon which he was encouraged with every grace imaginable, to stretch himself. Deftly she positioned him on his stomach, so that his face rested comfortably in a hole provided for that purpose. His legs were slightly parted allowing his penis to hang gently through another hole, his hands brought to rest palm-up beside him. Then she began to massage him. Within moments his body was in a state of relaxation he had never before experienced.

Tanya was evidently an expert at the art of sexual massage, and again he savoured her brand of temptation, as she only nearly touched where he desperately wanted her to touch. Warm oils were poured onto his body and gently rubbed all over; his back, his legs, into the crack of his bottom without the least hesitation or lingering sexual intimations. That was just another part of his body.

Then she began to massage. Kevin was lulled into a state bordering sleep by the wine, the soft motions of her hands, and the exotic surroundings. There was a point at which he couldn't have sworn he had not gone to sleep, but when his libido began to seriously awaken it was not because Tanya was stroking his penis, it was because she was not, and yet his whole body was aflame with desire. Alert once more, he began to move in soft co-ordination with her hands, and the pressure of her massage accommodated the change. Her hands slid to his buttocks and began kneading the flesh with circular movements. He began to will her fingers to move closer to his balls. He lifted himself slightly in the hope that her hands would slide there, but she simply moved with him, maintaining the pressure, the exquisite torture of withholding her touch.

There were times when Kevin was busting with need, and times when the pressure deflated, but never did the erotic pressure of that massage disperse. Subtly and with infinitesimal slowness her hands were working towards the core of his body, and Kevin's awareness followed her hands. There were times when he wanted to turn over and give her one, but deep inside he was waiting for the finale, desperate to know what it might be.

Then she began to massage the muscle that rimmed his anus. The action itself was almost enough to bring him to complete rampant erection – almost, but not quite. The very fact that he could have turned over and thrust himself into the bird of paradise massaging him was the whole reason he did not do so. Her hands promised delights he had never experienced, and he just didn't want it to stop.

Now her caressing finger was sliding just a fraction inside him. He groaned with frustration and delight, the two sensations intermingled inextricably, and it seemed that she dwelled at that point until he could have screamed.

Then her finger began to penetrate a little more at each circular movement, and he felt his penis had never been so fit to burst. It hung between his legs, throbbing and abandoned, while she played with his anus. He parted his legs slightly to accommodate, and at once her finger slipped right in. He jerked, gasped, and his hands clenched.

He was staring at the carpet, knowing he only had to lift his head to see her, but found he didn't want to. He knew what she was: a concubine from a harem, there but for no other purpose than to please him. It no longer mattered what she looked like; the important factor was whether she was doing nice things to him – and at that moment that was not in doubt.

Eventually he reached the stage where frustration was paramount, and again she seemed to anticipate this. All at once the teasing movement stopped. Her finger entered his body purposefully, and began to rub inside. Kevin felt every muscle in his body quiver into an exquisite tightness of expectation. He shivered and gasped like a man in the throes of a raging temperature. He felt seepage from his penis, and wished she would grasp it with her other hand. He almost lifted his hips so he could slip his own hands under his body, but almost in anticipation of his thoughts, her massaging increased in speed, leaving him floundering, legs widening in anticipation. Gradually the buzz built inside him and to his own surprise he knew he was going to ejaculate despite the fact that his penis had not been touched once. He stiffened, coalesced into one massive orgasm centred around whatever she was massaging in his anus, and spurted onto the carpet beneath his glazed eyes.

Then he collapsed, replete, and discovered that she was once again softly rubbing his body, not massaging, just gently revering his male wonderfulness. With that thought, he finally dozed off.

When he awoke a few minutes later he found Tanya kneeling before him, eyes attentive. She smiled softly.

'Is my master hungry now?' she asked sweetly.

To his surprise he was, and ambitions of further sex drifted amiably away. Boy, she had been good. But enough was enough. He rolled over, sat upon the couch, his feet dangling, and scratched happily at his crotch.

'Do you like Indian food?' she asked. 'My treat. But

first, stand up and turn around and cross your wrists.'

Somewhat amused, Kevin did as he was told. He had no objection to his wrists being tied, but if she thought he was going to get it up again in a while, she'd had it.

Once his wrists were tied she picked up a small length of red silk cord. 'Spread wide if you would, master.'

'What are you going to do?'

'In India this has a special name which, literally translated, means waiting in pleasure.'

'What does it do?'

'Would you like to find out?'

He shrugged, and would have been just as happy to have a description, but what the hell. 'Then do we go get some food?' he asked.

'As my master wishes.'

She knelt before him and took his empty balls in her hand, and wrapped a complicated knot around them which lifted and separated, and left two lengths of looped cord hanging. Utterly deflated by his most recent and wonderful orgasm, Kevin smiled slightly. Okay, it felt quite nice, but response was noticeably lacking.

'Now,' she said, 'if my master will come to the kitchen?'

He shrugged and followed. For some ancient Indian technique, the confinement was singularly uninteresting. In the kitchen she requested him to sit on a hard seat, his bound hands behind the tall back, his testicles hanging through a hole in the seat. She knelt beside him. 'My master's ankles?'

Now he realised what the dangling loops were for he almost balked, but she waited dutifully until he reached his ankles slowly towards her under the chair, and slipped his ankles into the loops provided before rising gracefully to her feet and over towards the kitchen worktop.

Kevin held his legs taut for a moment, then realised he was not going to be able to hold that tension for long, and relaxed slightly, allowing the cord to take the weight of his lower limbs. At once his testicles stretched down well below the seat. At first the sensation was uncomfortable rather than painful, but all too soon that changed.

He gritted his teeth and wondered how long he should put up with this torment before insisting she untied him.

He winced, wriggled, and lifted his legs, and the pressure released, but within moments his legs drooped again and the pressure under his crotch rose, pulling his testicles again. His bound hands clenched slightly as if they would assist in taking away the pressure, but he could reach nothing.

'Jesus!' he gasped after a moment. 'How long would a man in India be expected to sit like this?'

'As long as it takes, master,' she said ambiguously.

Sweat built up on his face as he wriggled around a bit more, lifting one buttock, then the other as he tried to find a comfortable spot. But the more he wriggled the more the strange pressure built up, the pain becoming almost excruciating. And yet, he had to concede that his penis had inflated just a tad.

Tanya was humming to herself, cutting small red peppers on a chopping board. He watched her, almost surprised that she was actually getting on and cooking a meal, having supposed that the sex bit over, they would probably just nip out for a take-away.

'Tanya?' he grunted.

'Yes, master?' The kohl-rimmed eyes assessed him over the veil.

'I think I'd like you to untie me.'

'If my master wishes.'

She glided forward, knelt between his legs, and bent her head into his lap. Unhesitatingly she lifted his penis to her mouth with her tongue and began to caress it, her hands reaching under the chair to slide up and down the back of his stretched balls. Kevin gasped at the unexpected action and froze, his hips arched towards her, another shot of blood pumping into his penis. As she licked an unnatural glow began to suffuse his nether regions. His hands clenched. Christ, she'd been chewing the chillies!

As his erection began to blossom, so the cord was no longer a pain, but an aphrodisiac. Now a finger was rubbing erotically against his anus, and to his surprise he again became fully erect, hard as a nail.

She looked up, her sloe eyes heavy-lidded. 'Does my master still wish to be untied?'

'Oh, shit no!' he gasped.

But instead of carrying on with her most wonderful fellatio, she stood up and went back to her curry. In went the meat and the colourful ingredients. Kevin was moving slightly, lifting one leg at a time to release the tension, each movement accompanied by a gasp as his prick and balls were pulled this way and that. After a few moments he closed his eyes and concentrated on surviving the excruciating experience. Was he supposed to stay like this until she had cooked the dinner? Was he expected to eat like this? He knew he couldn't. A groan escaped his lips.

With a flurry of silk she was there again, her hands

caressing his thighs, her lips enclosing his spearing tool. As she began to work on him he realised she was in total control. Although he moved fractionally to further enjoy her clever tongue, there was a point beyond which he could not move, and each time he reached it she would wait until he froze against his bonds before continuing her torturously delicate stimulation.

The pain of his constriction was all the more exquisite because he knew all he had to do was utter a single word and she would release him. But that was not the release he wanted. He felt the delicate rasp of her teeth against his throbbing helmet and thought he was about to explode. But still she stimulated him, her hands pressed against his hips to give herself the leverage she needed as she leaned down and sucked him in and out of her throat in long, languorous drafts. He held on as long as he could, his face going redder and redder as he held his breath with the effort, knowing the minute he relaxed he was going to lose it.

Then he allowed the orgasm to build. It started in his constricted testicles, cascaded outward in waves before flooding back to explode violently into Tanya's clutching throat. He wallowed in delicious ecstasy as he felt her muscles spasm as she swallowed.

As pleasure faded he realised he was now in extreme discomfort, but before he could make a single complaint, Tanya slipped his ankles free.

He leaned back in the chair, eyes closed, savouring the aftermath, and when he looked again Tanya was calmly putting the curry on the stove to simmer.

'What did you call that?' he asked at last, shuffling on

the seat to relieve the pressure on his balls.

She gave a cheeky grin, and said, 'My master can call it what he wishes.'

'Are you going to release me now?'

'If my master wishes it.'

'But?'

'I would like to feed my master and please him again.'

'Not possible,' he responded sadly.

She said nothing, but her eyes sparkled with amusement, and he realised that he had now come twice, and still had not seen the merest hint of a pussy.

Chapter Thirteen

Esther's upbringing had drummed into her the premise that to become sexually adventurous was some kind of convoluted first step down the long road to promiscuity. Instead, it was her valued judgement – mostly derived from personal experience – that lack of sexual awareness was more likely to lead to dissatisfaction and divorce. And yet even that discovery was not enough in itself to dissolve years of dogma. No, it was not simply the decision to do so, but the act of throwing aside her inhibitions that had been the huge hurdle, but slowly and surely that objective had been achieved. Now, every step forward was her own choice, as were the new boundaries to this freedom; quite simply, she could go as far as her own desires took her, and with whomever she wanted. However, despite the live subjects Madam used as teaching aids, and the enjoyable hours she spent tormenting them, her sole aim was to bring Kevin back into the fold and keep him there.

She made a cup of tea and took it in to Madam Tisset.

Madam Tisset leaned back on the comfortable sofa as she was wont, and sighed sorrowfully. 'Such a shame you don't want to come into the business – you're such a natural. Are you really sure you won't reconsider my offer?'

Esther giggled, bent down and kissed Madam's powdered cheek. 'I'm very flattered, but no. It's not what

I want to do with my life.'

'It's very lucrative, you know.'

'There's also a down side; there are some worrying people out there, and if I've learned one thing from you, it's that people are not so easy to categorise as I once thought. In fact, I'm stunned at how wrong I could be. That scares me a bit.'

'Reading a character comes with practice,' Madam Tisset persisted. 'Really it does. Men's eyes are windows to their souls. I don't have your fear of finding a bad one, because I know who they are.'

'Please, Madam Tisset, I've made up my mind.'

'Sorry. I did say I wouldn't try to persuade you, but it's in my nature.'

'I know.'

Madam Tisset became pensive for a moment, then leaned forward, a new glint in her eyes. 'Esther, all those frustrated ladies – ladies like you were – who just don't know how to enjoy sex properly. That's what you can do for me. Send me new clients. You'll know who they are: the ones who look at you with jealousy because they sense your inherent sexuality and don't know why they haven't got the same.'

'I can't do that!' Esther was aghast.

'Why not?'

'Once people knew what was going on I'd become an outcast and my husband would lose his job! You have no idea how small-minded people can be.'

'My dear, the less you say, the better. Just hint at how skilled you are at doing the things your husband loves, and how you owe it all to your old teacher. I guarantee the next thing you know you'll be asked – very, very discreetly, I can assure you – for my card. They won't even try to acknowledge it came from you; they will quietly get on with things and pretend to your face that nothing ever happened.'

Esther propped her chin on her hands, and her eyes narrowed as she viewed Madam Tisset with new respect. 'How many girls like me have you got out there handing your cards out to unsuspecting, frustrated housewives?' she asked.

Madam Tisset's eyes widened in abject innocence, a look she could achieve with little effort. 'Absolutely none like *you*, Esther. Really and truly.'

'You're a wicked woman!' Esther smiled.

'Yes, and isn't it fun?' Madam Tisset became more serious again. 'So, will you think about what I've proposed? Couldn't you think of it as a kindness to all the frustrated females out there with straying husbands? Just remember how much happier you are now than when you first came to me.'

Esther couldn't deny that she did feel happier for her visits, and the two women sat in silence for a few minutes.

'Now then,' Madam Tisset eventually said, 'I think it's time we furthered your education.'

'My education?'

'Yes, my dear. It's time you learned more about the world you've entered. I'm not talking about Kevin's fumbling attempts at domination. I'm talking about the real thing. Being out of control; strapped down, gagged, whipped, and sexually abused until you're screaming for more. Until you've really experienced it you can never know why people come to me, and why they come again and again.'

Esther fell silent once more, digesting this rather unexpected development. She realised that once again, Madam Tisset had managed to discover in her the ability to be embarrassed. 'Educated by you, you mean?'

'If you don't like that idea I can get a man in. I know a very good one. Bondage doesn't have to culminate in sex, even if a man is the dominant.'

'But I've never been beaten... I don't know—'

'I always insist on an escape word or sign. I don't allow anyone to say I've gone too far. You know that.'

Esther felt her cheeks burn. 'I don't think I can...'

For once Madam Tisset did not pressurise, but waited.

Esther dithered, realising that further taboos and boundaries were being crossed with this suggestion, and not only that, at a time she thought she had it all sussed out. Images of the men who'd been held in bondage here crossed her mind in a confused riot, each scenario becoming interspersed with her own erotic dreams.

Swallowing hard, she said, 'I – I think I'd rather someone I don't know did it. What do I have to do?'

Madam Tisset smiled warmly. 'Good girl,' she said. 'Go and shower, and I'll make a quick phone call.'

Esther could not enjoy the shower. Was she really going through with this? She tipped her head back and let the cascading hot water sting her cheeks, knowing she was putting off the time when she would have to climb out and face whatever awaited her.

There was a sheer dressing gown hanging on the back of the door, and once she'd dried herself she slipped it on.

The door opened and Madam Tisset wafted in. 'If you

would like to come with me?' she said.

Esther followed the woman through a corridor she had not visited before, and into a sterile room with a couch in the centre, above which hung a large light.

She shuddered with apprehension, more nervous than excited, hugging the robe around herself. She knew she was going to hate the whole experience. She was scared, exhilarated, but one thing she most adamantly was not, was sexually aroused. The moment some strange man laid his hands upon her she was going to scream blue murder and make all the 'no more' signs Madam Tisset had ever taught her. She just knew she was. She ought to go home.

'If you would just lay on the couch please, and get comfortable,' Madam Tisset cut into her thoughts. 'That's right – face down.'

Esther lay on the couch, hands by her side, rigid as a pole. The woman left, and as she did so the room filled with soothing music and Esther found herself drifting into a state bordering on sleep. The couch was very comfortable; the best way to lie was with her face pressed into the hole available, and as she began to relax the whole couch seemed to relax with her.

When the man finally arrived Esther lifted her head and stared curiously.

He was a mild man, not huge, but seemed pleasantly muscular beneath the white coat, and his fingers, she couldn't help noting, were long and artistic. She definitely had a thing about nice fingers.

'Please don't rise,' he said in a low, modulated tone. He pressed on her shoulder, stopping her from rising. She sank back down, feeling a slight sense of unease grip her.

But his hands were precise, reassuring, and she subsided beneath his expert touch as he continued.

'Now, first I'm going to relax your muscles with massage,' and as he spoke he pulled the flimsy gown from her shoulders and flipped it aside. Then he began to work.

And his hands were pure magic. They pressed hard up her back, buttocks to shoulders, swept outward and down to circle up again. As he worked, so she began to relax, to enjoy the lovely sensations. Never before had she ever been massaged, save when Kevin chose to scrub at her shoulders a couple of times at a pretence of relaxing her while he was already rampant and ready for a quick bonk.

It was too good and she didn't want it to stop. At what point she succumbed to the inevitable she was not sure; it was such a gradual process, so cleverly done.

He picked up one wrist and looped something around it. 'Just a small strap to hold it in place,' he said hypnotically. Then it was her other wrist, and then her ankles. And then, 'Just slip the head forward a mite. That's right, bite on the bar, that's what it's there for, to hold the head in the right position to work on the neck muscles. Now a little strap across the back of the head...'

Esther bit on the bar as instructed. It was somewhat uncomfortable, but before she could complain she was strapped into position, and that was that. Except that she could try the signal with her hands and see if he released her. But she didn't try it, for the rule was once you invoked the release you had to wait until another session. You couldn't just apologise and hope to carry on. It was one of Madam Tisset's inflexible rules.

He began to work again, caressing up and down her

body, discovering muscles she hadn't known existed. The skilled touch and her inability to move were very exciting. Because she could not rebel, as his hands began to glide closer and closer to her more sexual regions, she felt a rush of anticipation. He was becoming more intimate with each stroke. Caressing the fullness of her buttocks, round and round, causing her anus and the lips of her vagina to stretch with each encouraging movement.

Quite when she began to move with the flow of his hands, to indicate that, yes, she very much liked what he was doing, she wasn't sure. There was a kind of exhilaration; she was his prisoner, ergo, he could do what he wanted.

There came a time, however, when the massage was complete, and he surprisingly left the room. Esther found herself relaxing in the comforting hold of the couch, the music once again filling her mind. How long she was left there to enjoy the sensations she was not sure.

She sensed movement and tensed. She knew Madam Tisset and the man were both in the room.

The part of the couch her legs were strapped to separated and spread apart. She whimpered, exposed and vulnerable, but still she didn't make the sign.

They began to knead her body, to spread her buttocks. Lying face down she could indulge herself in the most exquisitely erotic sensations derived partially from enjoyment, derived almost wholly from the false premise that these two could do as they liked and she could not stop them. The fact that she could make the sign for which they were undoubtedly watching was neither here nor there. She groaned fractionally, her hips moving in time to the unknown hands that were caressing her buttocks and sliding closer and closer to her anus.

She held her breath at the unexpected touch and became almost paralysed, waiting for more. Was it the man? Was it her mentor? She didn't know, but the touch was exquisite, consuming her awareness, becoming more and more bold.

Then a rigid finger was pressing in, deeper and deeper, manipulating her muscle into compliance. She gasped, shuddered, but still did not request release. The finger began to tease, moving in and out at random, stretching her private passage, then slipping out to allow it to close. Then she felt something hard touch her there. It pressed, entered, stretched her further than the finger had, and exited again, beginning to move in gentle imitation of a penis. The extra stretch was exciting, excruciating, the unnatural entry filling her with shock. Each time the foreign object was pushed in it went a little further, and she guessed it must be the size and shape of a man's prick – it was a dildo. Because it was not real, however, it was no violation. No betrayal of Kevin, and she allowed herself to sink into the pleasure of this alien object penetrating her most vulnerable of orifices.

She could not talk, ask, request, demand; she could only accept or reject, each as final as the other. Therefore she was not surprised when the dildo – that or something else – was pushed one more time into her anus and began to expand. It got bigger and bigger until she was gasping for breath, on the verge of a scream, when the expansion stopped.

She breathed deeply, calming herself. Could she stand

it? She didn't make the sign for release and the expansion stayed within her, filling her bowels, consuming her mind.

By her sides her hands clenched and unclenched – though she didn't realise it – in the classic symptoms of masochistic enjoyment. Pain was pleasure. Please don't take away the pain. The balloon in her bowels was deflated and filled again. Then again. She winced at every tiny movement, every muscle in her body moving in time with the experience, and there came a time when she no longer thought about trying to make the sign that would release her. She simply existed in this body, this pain-and-pleasure-filled body.

At that point she was left alone to wallow in the experience. At first she had no idea she was alone, then the soft music and lack of movement in her peripheral vision informed her that she had probably been alone for a while.

Her bottom throbbed and contracted, trying to eject the foreign object, but it would not be rejected. Instead the whole stretched feeling began to filtrate to the single place between her legs where her own private pleasure lay. She wanted to put her fingers between her legs, to induce a giant orgasm which would flood her with relief, yet the bondage held her in thrall to the experience. She had no choice but to lie under the strange sensations that filled her, and to become more and more frustrated by her lack of control.

When she sensed movement in the room her reaction was one of hope that they would allow her to bring herself off. She could not move her head to see who it was, but she ached with expectation.

That was when the first lash of the whip bit into her vulnerable buttocks.

She recoiled with an anguished cry. When the next stroke landed she was more under control and managed to take the blow without wincing quite so hard. To her shock some small part of her brain analysed the procedure; pictured her lying there, and was horrified. But the deeper side of her psyche, a side she had never before encountered, told her the experience was wonderful. With each stroke of the whip, or whatever was landing like liquid fire on her sensitised skin, her bowels contracted around the foreign object, trying to eject it. Christ, she was so out of control it was good. If only she could touch...

The blows landed on her buttocks again and again until she could no longer determine the point of contact, her skin flaming into a single entity, and yet the pleasure sensors in her brain wallowed, writhed, exhilarated in the torment. All she wanted to do was to orgasm, but she couldn't touch herself.

Now she didn't care who was hitting her. She groaned and endured, enjoyed, and still the blows rained on her flushed skin until her body felt to be on fire. Her imagination lent a vivid picture of welts and weals that were purple as they crossed in a latticework. When the blows stopped she was almost unaware of it. Lost in the contemplation of self, cessation of pain was almost a pain in itself. She felt a body press into the gap between her open legs, and felt a hand reach between her legs. Oh, *yes*...

She began to move. A finger inserted itself just where it should be and began to move. She moved in rhythm. If it was the man, yes please, he could enter. Disappointingly no penis thrust between her legs – but the finger moved faster over her bud. It was doing the things she liked most. She groaned and willed it to move faster until she was aflame, the fire spreading through her in waves of ecstasy over which she had no control...

Then it was over.

She gasped against the bar that propped her mouth open, and scarcely noticed when the intrusion was removed from her anus. Then Madam Tisset gently rubbed her back, which was beginning to throb uncomfortably, with cooling unguent, and she sank into lethargic sexual aftermath, sleepily wallowing in selfish contemplation which verged on sleep.

Later, when Madam Tisset removed the bonds, led her to the shower, and handed her her own clothes, she was strangely quiescent, like a child being told what to do. It was only afterwards when she was dressed and sitting in stunned comprehension on Madam Tisset's settee, that she was able to take full stock of what had happened.

'Now do you understand?' Madam Tisset said gently.

Esther was hardly able to whisper her reply. 'Yes... yes I do.'

Chapter Fourteen

The latest banking function grew closer, but Esther felt surprisingly guilty about her recent behaviour and not really interested. Kevin kept throwing her the odd questioning glance. This made her feel as though her experiences with Madam Tisset and her new sexual freedom had pushed her down the sordid road to self-gratification, and that he suspected something. Despite his own frequent infidelities, she was almost driven to tell him the whole truth.

Yet some sense of self-preservation warned her to say nothing; time would not be turned back, and whatever transpired in the future, her innocence was lost for good.

The evening of the dinner arrived, and Esther dutifully put aside her own needs to assist in her husband's meteoric rise within the firm. The big boss gave a broad smile as she and Kevin entered the dining room, standing to welcome them with a nauseating familiarity. She smiled brightly, allowing Kevin to remove the cape from her shoulders, and many surreptitious glances eagerly devoured the classy but sexually mouth-watering vision.

She smiled graciously and mingled amongst the gaggle of wives, accepting their haughty niceties with elegant ease and politeness.

Kevin watched the men, and thoroughly enjoyed being

the husband of an alluring wife, proud of her blatant sexuality. Quite what had transpired to perform the miracle he was not quite sure, but suspected it had something to do with those evening classes she seemed to like so much. He would like to meet the lady that ran them one day, to thank her.

Throughout the evening the other women looked sour, the men buzzed around Esther like the proverbial bees, and she simply sparkled. Kevin spent the evening feeling incredibly proud of her, and incredibly put out by the attention she was attracting. He was strangely torn. One moment he felt like a pimp accepting eagerly that she should flaunt herself for his own advancement, then like a heel for the same reason, then furious with her for flirting so brazenly.

As the evening progressed his pride soured to jealousy: she was acting like a bitch in heat. She was chasing anything in trousers because she was no longer satisfied with him. Perhaps she was quietly working her way out of their marriage. He didn't drink alcohol because he was driving, so by the time they were going home he was sober and angry.

Without warning he swung the car into a lay-by and screeched to a halt.

'Wuh-what's wrong?' Esther stammered, wrenched from her dozing by the sudden yank of her seatbelt.

'Everything's wrong,' he snapped, pulling the handbrake on viciously. 'What are you trying to do, ruin me? Acting like a bloody whore with all my colleagues and bosses!'

'Oh, don't be so infantile!' she snapped.

'You're acting like a whore, and I don't understand why.

You were never like this before.'

'But I thought you wanted me to be like this? I thought the idea was that I help you go up in the world. And let's face it, this is about the only way you will!' She had drunk fairly liberally, and the scathing words poured out uncensored.

Kevin was astounded. She had never said such things to him before. 'So you're flaunting yourself for my advancement?' he said quietly. 'I – I was doing okay anyway, thank you very much.'

'You were getting nowhere fast, except in bed with your secretary,' she retorted nastily, irritated that all her hard work was being belittled in such a fashion.

'Oh, I see,' he said. 'So you're getting your own back. Why didn't I guess?'

'What's good for the goose is good for the gander,' she went on relentlessly. 'Okay, so I like the men to look at me. It makes me feel good. It makes me feel sexy. I'm not going to apologise for that.'

'You whore.'

'Perhaps, but I'm whoring for you, you ungrateful moron.'

'So you admit it?' he said, his fight returning. 'You've been with other men?' Until he voiced the accusation he hadn't really thought it. He was astounded at the guilt written all over her face. Slowly, at the realisation of her infidelity, he unclipped his seatbelt. Esther flinched at the anger etched on his face as he climbed out of the car, walked around the front through the beams of the headlights, and pulled her door open.

Then she was frightened. She'd overstepped the mark.

This was getting out of hand. 'Kevin... Kevin I didn't do—'

'Get out!' he snarled.

'Kevin, you're scaring me!'

'That,' he assured her nastily, 'is the general idea. Now, get out before I drag you out!'

She slipped out, standing uncertainly in the moonlight by the side of the car. Was he going to leave her there? He was staring at her very strangely.

'You beautiful whore,' he whispered, shaking his head sadly as he gathered a tow rope from the boot. 'Walk away from the car. You want a sexual fantasy? I'm going to give you one you won't forget in a hurry.'

He stepped towards her, a hand raised threateningly. She backed away, shocked by his cold aggression. They were on the edge of a park notorious for muggings. Was he going to leave her there? No, as she backed away uncertainly on heels not suited to uneven ground, so he followed.

When they were a distance from the car Kevin said, 'This will do.'

She whimpered as he grabbed her. Still unbelieving and faintly trusting, she struggled without any real effort against his strange actions as he wound the rope around her wrists. 'Kevin,' she said meekly, 'what are you doing? Kevin?'

'Shut up.' He threw the rope over a thick branch of a tree and pulled, stretching her arms up and her face in against the trunk. Then he secured the rope. 'Now you'll get what you've been asking for, you sex-hungry bitch,' he said. Her feet scrambled against the grass and slippery roots, trying to take the weight from her arms.

'Kevin, let me down...'

He reached beneath her dress, yanked down her panties and sheer tights with a single tug, and roughly removed them from her feet. Her heeled shoes gone, she was stretched on tiptoe, almost hanging from the end of the creaking rope. She whimpered. He stuffed her panties into her mouth and tied the tights around to hold it in place. Her wails became a wordless moan. Then to her horror she heard his footsteps disappearing up the bank behind her. Stretched tightly against the trunk she couldn't even turn her head to follow as he scrambled off into the darkness.

She didn't believe he had really done it until she heard the car start and drive away. She moaned deep in her throat. She was in a park where strange men were known to wander, strung up against a tree without even her knickers for protection. She was an open invitation for the next man who came along.

The warm glow of the dinner party had long since faded. She shivered. She pulled desperately at the rope, but her wrists were butted together in a neatly whipped bracelet pulled even tighter by a tensioning loop between them, and her own weight did the rest, holding the knot firmly in place.

She tried to get her feet around the trunk, to take the weight from her wrists to try to loosen the knot, but the trunk was too wide. She tried to haul herself up on the rope to remove the gag with her hands, but her arms, never strong, refused to obey her desperate commands.

A rising night breeze began to chill her thighs, and as

she realised that the involuntary stretching must have lifted the dress to the point of displaying her lack of underwear, she whimpered hopelessly, clamping her legs together coyly. She tried to call for help through the gag, but her vulnerability soon gave rise to second thoughts. Perhaps she really didn't want to do that. If she stayed nice and quiet, till daylight, perhaps then would be a safer time to attract attention.

She struggled to look around, but could see little beyond the tree trunk. It was a dark night. In the distance there was the haze of streetlights, the hum of an occasional car, and high above was the twinkling of little stars. Never had she felt so alone. For a moment she accepted that she was helpless, then she grew angry. How dare he do this to her? How dare her husband leave her at the potential mercy of muggers or tramps? After all, the way she'd behaved at the dinner was hardly in the infidelity league tables to which he belonged.

She wriggled and pulled, trying to swing her feet up to the branch above her head, and was aware of her totally exposed bottom as she futilely attempted this gymnastic feat. Then, immediately she attempted a particularly energetic manoeuvre, there was a horrible tearing of cloth.

Her feet dropped to the damp earth and a cold chill chased up her spine. Then, behind her, she heard the sound of footsteps approaching, and froze.

She held her breath and pretended she was invisible, but a wheeze of indrawn breath told her she had been noticed. Oh no, she was some pervert's dream come true. Or perhaps there was such a thing left in the world as a gentleman? Perhaps he would untie her, cover her with his coat, and carry her off to safety. She remained still and listened. He was there. She could hear him breathing. How she knew it was a man she couldn't say, but it was. She prayed he would let her go.

She tried again to look over her shoulder, but could see nothing except shadows. Yet he was there. She could feel his breath now, on her shoulder. She whimpered hopelessly.

Hands gingerly touched her back. She wrenched at the bonds, moaning into the gag. There was a hiss of fear. The hands withdrew as if stung. She tensed and waited, then the hands came creeping back. Softly and surely they began to seek out her white flesh in the darkness.

Esther tried to turn, to see the nature of her tormentor, but his hands gripped her hair, stopping any movement. He held her there for a moment, as if thinking, then she heard a slithering noise, followed by the feel of a strip of silky fabric being wound twice around her eyes and tied off. Probably his tie, she reasoned, and if so, this was no simple tramp, but a man who had every intention of taking what was on offer, and no intention at all of being recognised. Perhaps it was someone she'd recognise. Perhaps he knew who she was...

The man said nothing. He just took. He stood behind her and touched her, his seeking hands gradually becoming more bold at her obvious immobilisation. He touched her everywhere. Esther wriggled, struggled, and moaned, but still the hands mauled her. They burrowed inside her dress and sought her breasts. She sucked in a muffled gasp as fingers teased her nipples beneath the material. He then put a knee between her legs, holding her there, spreading his legs to force hers apart. Even through his trousers she could feel heat radiating from his groin, and felt an undeniable flicker of response in her own body as he moved gently against her.

Then, having thoroughly explored her breasts, his hands slid downward, stretching her expensive dress out of shape to caress her abdomen, her soft bush of hair, and tease at the opening between her legs. He grunted. The hands withdrew. Esther moaned slightly with regret, hardly aware that she did so. Then his hands slid onto her flesh once more. As he caressed her thighs the dress was pushed up slowly and sensuously over her hips to expose her body more fully to his seeking hands.

The fact that she wasn't being hurt by the opportunist had by now penetrated Esther's fear, giving way to more primitive sensations. The unknown man's hands were gentle, doing all the right things, and as her body began to respond to his caresses, his fingers slid to the moist lips beneath her bush and teased gently, surely, at the entrance which was stretched and available through the pressure of his legs. She moaned with approval, moving hopefully against his fingers as his groin ground against her bottom with increasing urgency.

Then his hands slid back and she heard the rasp of a zipper, and a gasp of relief. She felt knuckles on the cheeks of her bottom as the unknown man touched himself with evident enjoyment, while pressing his thumb on the puckered knot of her anus. As she writhed against him he clearly recognised the invitation, and pressed his thumb in, causing her to shudder with delight at the rude invasion. Gently her violator eased his thumb in and out, teasing the opening into further compliance, and she knew what was to come. He pulled her thighs, forcing her legs further apart, and she felt the warmth of his erection press insistently against her exposed backside. He nibbled at her neck and ears, moving back and forth.

Esther groaned with frustration as the heat of his rod slid between her legs, teasing, touching, but not penetrating, and she began to make soft mewling noises. Quite when her struggles turned into gyrations of delight she would not have been able to say with accuracy. All she knew was there came a time when she wanted his penis inside her more than anything, and when she writhed against him in frustration, unable to speak, to cajole him into doing what she so desperately wanted him to do. Her own lack of control was an erotic stimulus she was beginning to recognise.

The stranger had said nothing, but she could feel his breath quicken, his erection pulse warmly against her flesh, teasing at both entrances, now one, now the other, wetting them further with his own lubricant. She shuddered with absolute sexual desire. She wanted to feel this man's penis inside her. The whole evening had been fraught with sexual innuendoes, with hints and oblique invitations, and now the added stimulus of her bondage turned Esther into a creature of the night. She didn't give a damn who was with her, all she knew was this was what she wanted.

The man seemed to sense the change in her. He pulled her legs apart further with his hands around her inner thighs, and pushed his erection firmly against her arse. She gasped with anticipation as he pushed gently but surely against the constriction. Her anus gradually and reluctantly opened to accommodate the full girth of him. Then he stopped pushing, and she realised she was fully impaled upon him. For a moment they were still, and she could think of nothing save the pulsing rod thrust up inside her, stretching the ring of her bottom tightly around its base.

Then he began to move, just slightly. Her muscle spasmed against him, her whole body responded. She heard him groan. Hands pushed the dress further up, exposing her to his needs. He ground her nipples between his fingers, splayed his hands over her breasts, her abdomen, then began to rub her between the legs as he buggered her.

Expertly, he rubbed. He knew where and how. She thrashed and heaved against him, still impaled, while he steadily brought her to a massive and uncontrollable orgasm, and as she came so did he, and as he did so he leaned into her neck and groaned, 'Oh, *honey*...'

Esther froze. He did it. He bloody did it!

She gave a little squeal of surprise as he withdrew, prompting another of those strange spasms as she closed tightly behind him. Then she waited. She heard his breathing begin to slow, and heard the sound of his zipper being raised.

Her dress was still rucked up, and the chill of the night was once more penetrating the euphoria of her sexual encounter. She tugged on the rope, wanting release, but Kevin gave her a smart rap on the bare backside, and mumbled, 'Thanks, sweetie, nice arse.' Then the dress was heaved back down.

Then she was left in silence. The bastard! He'd walked away and left her there. She screamed her anger into the gag, and waited.

What else could she do?

After a moment she became frightened. She was getting cold and her arms ached. Then, from behind her came the hasty sound of steps. Oh no, who this time? Then arms wrapped around her and she realised it was Kevin as he began to apologise, crying into her shoulder, telling her he hadn't meant to hurt her, hadn't meant to leave her there on her own for so long.

Once the gag was removed she wondered whether Kevin was waiting to hear her admit what had happened, or whether she was simply supposed to keep silent after guessing it was him. Then she realised the truth: he was scared to admit what he'd done, afraid she would be so shocked she would hate him forever. And if she admitted she knew it was him, surely that would have the same effect? He was expecting her to keep quiet.

It was at that moment she realised it was Kevin who had been keeping her innocent all these years. The more he played around, the more he had put her on a pedestal, separating her in his mind as something more pure than the other women he went out with, yet at the same time wishing he could do to her all the things he did to those others.

As he untied her and took her home and to bed, she realised he was reacting from guilt, ashamed of himself for using her in that way. She also realised she was in a bit of a quandary: damned if she said she knew it was him, damned if she didn't. She frowned. All that learning at Madam Tisset's hands and she couldn't put it to use. She could not even tell him how exquisitely wonderful his lovemaking had been, and how she would very much like him to do it again, because Kevin didn't want her off her pedestal, he didn't want her to be human enough to have enjoyed it, damn him.

Lying in bed, listening to him gently snoring, she realised that this all had to come to a head, and soon. She had accepted her sexuality, and so must Kevin. One thing she could not do was slip back into being a frustrated housewife. Oh no, things had gone far beyond that.

Chapter Fifteen

The letter came through the door with the rest of the post, but something about it made Kevin slip it into his pocket for later perusal.

It burned a hole in his pocket all the way into work, and in the privacy of his office, with all the stealth of a cold-war spy, he slit open the envelope and pulled out a white card. Bemused, he stared at the embossed, flowery writing.

If you would like to be dominated by an expert, call me.

He turned the card over. On the back was an address, a telephone number, and the scribbled words: *I'm waiting for you.*

The signature looked like Tisser, or something, he couldn't quite make it out. Grimacing, he thrust the card in his pocket and got on with his work, pausing only now and then to reflect on the strange missive. He couldn't recall having a fling with a woman by the name of Tisser, not that he was much in the habit of recalling the names of his many conquests at all. After a month or so they tended to melt into a pot of fleshy memories. As far as sex was concerned, he lived only for the present, and really had no interest in some old fling trying to wheedle her way into his life. And yet this mysterious card excited him in a way he could not describe. To be dominated had not been his intention at all, and he'd had no idea it could so absolutely consuming until the day he'd been kidnapped by the lady in black. Of course! That was what it was about! How stupid he'd been. The memories triggered, bringing his libido flooding to life.

Having given him a dose of her extreme sexuality, she was now seeing if he would come to her, and that meant she was a professional. Hell, he had no intention of getting into that never-ending money pit when sex was freely available all around him, just for a little effort on his part. Yet he recalled, with vivid clarity, the anguish of his captivity combined with the most intense sexual experience of his life. And a strange thought seeped into his mind: what would she charge? Again and again he denied that he wanted to see her, and tried to tell himself that he liked submissive females, and yet the card played havoc with his equanimity and fired his imagination until he was aflame with curiosity.

Just once wouldn't hurt, would it?

The guilt he'd been harbouring over buggering his wife was already fading. Esther had said nothing about it, and it became obvious to him that she'd buried the memory by reverting to her normal placid self. Perhaps now he should persuade her to stay that way. She was his wife, after all, not some whore. With a resolve of self-sacrifice, he decided he should forgo the rapid escalation of his career to have Esther back well and truly where she belonged – at home as a housewife.

Almost absently he fingered the card in his pocket, and by late afternoon he had actually pored over his street map to determine the location of the address, and discovered it to be in a seedy part of town. Not a place anyone respectable could be found, certainly not any of his work colleagues, and that clinched it for him.

He would see the enigmatic woman – whoever she was – one more time, and that was that. Absolutely and finally. In a no-nonsense mood, and with his best banker's voice filled with all the superiority he could muster, he called the number on the card. It was answered instantly in a cultured, polite manner, which he had not expected.

'Madam Tisset's residence, can I help you?'

'I've been sent me a card,' he said positively. 'I'm phoning to make an appointment.'

'And when would sir like to visit?'

'Um, tomorrow morning?'

'And who shall I say is calling?'

He paused for a moment, thrown slightly. 'Um, Sam... Sam Weatherall.'

'Fine, eleven-thirty okay?'

'Eleven-thirty?' Now he was committing himself his heart started to pound. 'Yeah, I guess so.'

'Good, that's booked in then. We look forward to seeing you tomorrow, Sam.'

'How—?' he was about to ask how much it would cost, but the line clicked dead. The cost didn't matter that much, anyway. He put the phone down slowly. Had he really booked himself in for a session with a prostitute? It was hard to believe that the pleasant girl at the other end of the phone line wasn't a doctor's receptionist or something like that. Perhaps he had it all wrong. Perhaps it was a bona fide therapeutical practice with no 'extras'. Surely prostitutes didn't employ receptionists?

He shook his head, put it all to the back of his mind, and got on with his work. He didn't have to keep the appointment anyway, because this Madam Tisset person had no idea who had really called.

Next morning Kevin bumbled around in the office, hardly aware that he was doing no work at all. The anticipation of what lay in store had set his heartbeat to a rapid rate, his pulse thudding.

It was her, his mystery woman, he just knew it was.

Just to be on the safe side he parked the car a few streets away and walked to the address on the card. The building was an old red brick affair which must have once been a warehouse, and some of the windows were either barred or bricked-in. Not a particularly salubrious place.

He pressed the bell, and the door opened.

'Hello, Sam,' welcomed a very matronly woman. 'Please come in.'

He balked slightly – she was a bit old – then stepped inside. She closed the front door and he followed her up a narrow dingy staircase.

To his relief he was shown into a white room which might have been that of a dentist or doctor. Everything looked very clean and professional.

'The shower is in there,' she said, pointing, 'and you'll find a robe on the back of the door. If you would like to freshen up then come back in here.'

Showered and already feeling nicely relaxed, Kevin had to wait for a few minutes until the woman returned.

'Now Sam,' she said, 'what we would like to do is get you absolutely relaxed. To aid this process and stop anything from causing distraction, sensory deprivation will be instigated for just a few moments. All this means is that you will put a blindfold on, use the headphones, and listen to calming music while you rest.'

She drew him to the side of the massage table and put a small pair of earphones on him. The room was instantly distanced by a soft sound which could have been a mixture of heavy breathing and the sound of sea washing an exotic shore. She then handed him a silk blindfold with straps, which he put in place himself. As her hands guided him to the bench, where he lay face down, she also loosened the robe so that the couch was in direct contact with his skin, and as he instantly calmed, arms by his sides, she slipped it from him totally.

A small part of his mind was analysing the softening process, equating it with what he did to prospective clients, and he had to admit it was working very well. When hands very softly began to rub oil on his back he was not worried at all, far from it, he had decided to enjoy the experience. As the masseuse – he assumed it was this Madam Tisser – began to work, he detected the hands of an expert. He relished the persistent smoothing of hands up his spine, easing the strands of muscle slowly but surely into a state of absolute relaxation. She was good. As she caressed and her hands gently moved his buttocks in circles the inevitable happened; his penis very gradually but surely began to grow. He moved subtly to accommodate it, but lying face down was not the best way to deal with the problem. As though the masseuse knew this was happening her hands roved more insistently to the muscles at the tops of his thighs, manipulating the flesh this way and that, stretching his buttocks. Kevin realised she must know he was aroused, and her actions were becoming more and more erotic, teasing, and the relaxation tape had become slightly more vibrant. Now it definitely sounded like a woman panting with desire.

Then the earphones were removed and a sultry voice whispered, 'Hello, Sam. I am Madam Tisset. You may call me Madam. Have you enjoyed the session so far?'

'I – er – yes... Madam.'

'Now, you know I'm a professional dominant, and will do my best to give you the most satisfying session you have ever had. This will include pleasure -- and a certain amount of pain.' A finger glided down his back, and he knew he was not to lift his head or remove the blindfold. 'If you do not want this, you now have your last opportunity to leave.'

There was only the sound of his breathing in the silence.

'Good boy, Sam,' she purred. 'Now, I will give you a release sign. If the first two fingers on both hands cross simultaneously, the session will be terminated instantly at that point. Show me you understand.'

He crossed the required fingers as her finger slipped between his buttocks and caressed just around his balls. He gasped at the sudden flood of sexual craving he experienced.

'Good boy,' she purred hypnotically. 'Now, a single word of warning. You will answer my questions politely, and deny me nothing. If you deny me in any way whatsoever I will terminate the session. If you cross your fingers I will terminate the session. If the session is terminated you will pay the full fee and leave the premises the instant you are dressed. Do you understand?'

'Yes,' he whispered.

'Madam.'

'Yes, Madam,' he corrected.

'Very well. Turn over. I wish to shave you.'

Shave him? What would Esther say? He opened his mouth, then closed it again, and turned over in the darkness of the blindfold.

'Oh my, you have been enjoying yourself, haven't you?' she chided.

'Yes, Madam, I'm afraid I have.'

'Good. Now, spread slightly.'

There was a soft warmth of shaving cream, and a blade began to clear away the coarse hair around his genitals. His fingers clenched the sides of the couch and his erection rose powerfully. The scraping feeling was wonderful, but not nearly as erotic as the touch of her hand upon his newly shorn flesh as she smoothed it, checking for stubble. Then the whole area was washed again, and talcum powder applied.

'That's better,' she concluded. 'Now get up. That's right. Give me your hand. There are no steps.'

She led him forward and he followed, his step hesitant.

She made him stand still, then requested one hand. He held it out, and felt her wrap a thick leather restraint around it. His penis throbbed excitedly at the sensation. She requested his other hand, then his ankles, one after the other. Then she took the blindfold from him.

They were standing in a room filled with contraptions of all sorts. A huge wheel with restraints, various benches, stools, stocks, and many things he was hardly able to comprehend a use for. But the most terrifying and impressive sight was the implements which surrounded him, on all the walls. Implements designed for all kinds of bondage and sexual torture. He shivered. What was he doing here?

Glancing down at his own ankles and wrists he realised the restraints he wore were now attached to two poles on each side of him by chains. At the moment he could reach to undo them himself, but if the ratchets spread him to full stretch, he would be immobilised totally. She stood behind him, and he began to turn his head to see her.

'Stop!'

The authority in her tone made him freeze. 'Well, little man, how brave do you feel?' she taunted. 'Will you release yourself and walk away, or shall I carry on?'

He gritted his teeth against her patronising. 'Carry on,' he snapped.

A small motor began to whine and the chains attached to his wrists slid up inside the poles. He winced, but found his wrists being drawn inexorably upwards and out. Then they stopped moving, and as the pitch of the motor changed the chains on his ankles began to tighten. He shuffled his feet further and further out until his legs were parted at a stretch that was a tad beyond comfortable. Then his wrists were pulled once more until he stood in an enforced star shape. His hands wrapped around the chains and clenched hard.

He sensed movement, and his tormentor walked into his vision, clutching an impressive whip. He gaped. It was not his dream dominant at all, but the woman who had let him in, only now she was dressed in a tightly laced leather bodice. She wore stockings, and her high-heeled boots were laced up to the knee. He was shocked. Surely a woman of her age should have a little more decency?

A glint in her eye told him she knew exactly what he was thinking. She moved closer, her hips rolling, and he found her movements surprisingly sexual and very feminine. With the handle of the whip she lifted his limp penis. 'Is that all you can manage?' she teased. 'Do you want me to do nice things to this rather charming body of yours, and give it a little helping hand?'

'I'm not sure this is—' Kevin halted abruptly as she drew back her arm, took aim, and swept the tip of the whip expertly against one thigh. He yelled and leapt, insofar as he could within his bonds.

'You're supposed to say yes, please, Madam,' she warned, glancing up at his hands.

He realised she was looking for signs that he was going to wimp out. 'Yes please, Madam,' he said through gritted teeth, torn between saying no and crossing his fingers.

She smiled, a feline curl of the lips. 'Very well, Sam. Now you've seen your surroundings and are suitably impressed, I'm going to blindfold and gag you again. Then I'm going to tie a weight to your balls and beat you. Then I'm going to leave you to enjoy that for a while before continuing. Do you understand?'

'Yes, Madam,' Kevin said, almost surprising himself.

She smiled knowingly, and went to the wall. She chose a hood with an integral gag and went back to him. Leaving himself so emotionally and physically exposed to a woman made him feel as though he was betraying his masculinity and belittling himself, but he obediently opened his mouth and let her slip the lump between his lips and the hood over his head. Locked into darkness once more, he felt her tweak it all into place and buckle it up tight. Somehow he felt more comfortable in the dark, like a child imagining he couldn't be seen because he couldn't see others. And though he knew where he stood and what was around him, the darkness distanced him from his own inhibitions.

She deftly strapped something around his balls. His buttocks tightened as a finger, inadvertently or otherwise, brushed against his anus, increasing both his senses of vulnerability and sexual awareness. All he knew were the strange sensations of constriction, and suddenly the stretching and pulling of a weight on his scrotum. He gasped around the gag, winced at the bizarre sensation, then gradually the weight increased as she lowered the full weight.

As the burden settled between his spread thighs Kevin realised he was revelling in his thraldom, and he waited in delicious anticipation for her to complete the rest of her promise. He no longer cared that she was of an age that would not normally interest him.

Without warning the bite of the whip caught him on his thigh and he jerked like a puppet in his bonds. The further pain of the weight moving gradually stilled to a dull ache, and when the whip descended again he concentrated on curtailing his movements as much as possible. Then the bite of the whip landed more regularly. It attacked his thighs and buttocks, then began to seek out more sensitive targets: his nipples, his anus, and the exposed tip of his penis. At first the pain was paramount, each stroke causing him to writhe and groan, then gradually pain suffused his body to the extent that the pain itself was an aphrodisiac, and gradually he felt the stiffening and tightening of his cock as it began to grow once more. Why it happened he had no idea, but after a while his whole awareness became focused on the sensations of his body. He was no longer a man, no longer a banker, no longer an individual.

He simply was.

He waited, not knowing when the next stroke was going to bite. After a while he realised he was alone, just as she'd promised, with only his bondage, his scorched flesh, and the exquisite discomfort of the gently swinging weight to occupy his spinning thoughts.

And in the darkness he waited, his fingers clenched tight and his flesh bathed in sweat.

Chapter Sixteen

Esther was quietly amused that Kevin could have gone through the whole experience and come home to her pretending he had simply been at work. But then again, he would be equally shocked if he knew she had been there, watching Madam Tisset at work. She decided it was about time all the deception was taken out of the equation.

But only two days later Kevin phoned her at home. 'Sorry, honey,' he said, 'it's this big meeting I have to prepare for. I'm going to be working so late I thought I'd better stay in the city tonight. I knew you'd understand. Love ya.'

'Love you, too,' she said, and replaced the handset thoughtfully.

Two years ago she would have believed him. A year ago she would have pretended to believe him. But not any more.

It took ten phone calls before she discovered the hotel into which he was booked. He hadn't even bothered to use a false name. A double room for a night and champagne, the receptionist told her with bright enjoyment. It was lovely to see a man interrupting a heavy working week to remember his wife on their wedding anniversary. So romantic.

'Romantic my arse,' Esther said to herself, and deliberately burned a hole in the trousers she was ironing.

Then she carefully put the iron down, switched it off, and picked up the receiver again.

When she replaced it, Kevin would have been horrified to see the malicious amusement on her normally placid face.

Esther had had an accident, they said on the telephone, and was at the hospital. He'd left work in a total panic and scoured the emergency wards – but to no avail. Esther was not there. By the evening he had visited three hospitals in varying degrees of agitation and an increasing suspicion that it was a very nasty practical joke.

Where was she? No one knew.

Who had called in to report the accident? No one knew.

He had driven twice across the city, and between frustrating attempts to communicate with the hospital staff, who must surely have been interviewed for personality and presentation by an ageing orang-utan with an attitude problem. He had tried to phone home, but there had been no answer.

Someone at work was going to pay for this damned joke, he decided. He seethed with tiredness, frustration and righteous anger because he had paid for the hotel room in advance, and the joker had cost him a day's holiday and the hotel fee, not to mention a little session with Gloria.

But even though he finally decided that the planned entertainment for the evening was also out; he had to make sure Esther really was all right. As he swung his car out towards the suburbs he also tried to phone Gloria to put her off, but her mobile wasn't answering. Damn! He'd told her to leave it on so he could contact her.

Sure enough, when he arrived home Esther was on the sofa looking crumpled and surprised. She held a half-read paperback. 'I thought you were working late?' she said.

'I finished up early, honey,' he said, kissing her on the cheek, feeling more relieved than he would have thought possible to find his wife her normal placid and understanding self.

'You've been working too hard,' she said with plenty of concern. 'You've got that drawn look you always get when you're tired.'

He blushed a little guiltily, deciding not to tell her about the spiteful practical joke, and to play on her sympathy instead. 'Yeah, well, perhaps I have.'

'Well, you go and get in the bath and relax. I'll bring you up a beer.'

He shrugged. Why not? There was certainly nothing better to do now, and all thoughts of sex had totally dissipated. What a let down, after what he'd planned for the night.

He sank back in the lovely hot bath, however, and accepted Esther's wifely ministrations as his due, while dreaming of the luscious Gloria and pondering the injustices of life.

Esther brought him up his favourite beer, and then left him to it. As he lay back and closed his eyes and thought of Gloria's delicious tits his cock swelled in the gently lapping water, and he gripped it dreamily in his fist. He began to gently massage himself beneath the warm water, and gradually his annoyance at missing out on what promised to be a memorable night faded as he drifted to the realms where fantasy met flesh…

But he was wrenched back to reality with a start as Esther suddenly bustled in.

'Wh-what do you want?' he snapped abruptly, a little water slopping over the side of the bath as he tried to quickly conceal his semi-erect cock beneath his hands and struggled to sit up.

'Oh,' she looked a little taken aback by his aggressive outburst, 'I'm just going to pop over to Jenny's house. I promised her a recipe, and I'll probably stop for a coffee. I won't be more than an hour or so.'

'Fine,' he said, wishing he hadn't snapped at her. After she'd gone got back to the job in hand. Eventually he lifted his hips, closed his eyes, every ounce of awareness sucked into the expectancy of the pleasure which throbbed between his legs. 'Oh,' he gasped. 'Oh, nearly, nearly!'

'Mmm,' he heard from behind him. 'That's nice.'

For the second time Kevin let go abruptly and his eyes flew open. He sat up again, sploshing more water over the side, intensely annoyed at having his pleasure summarily cut short, words of admonishment on his lips.

But even as he turned he knew the woman who leaned nonchalantly in the doorway was not Esther. She wore a short dress of something lacy, through which black satin underwear, sheer black stockings and suspender belt were displayed to advantage, as was the enticing bulge of her breasts and the flat expanse of her middle. Green eyes glittered through a sequinned hood.

'I wouldn't do that if I were you,' she said.

'What the hell...?' he began, horrified, and lunged to his feet, his sexual urge forgotten in the sudden panic.

She stood up straight and her voice hardened. 'Esther

will be a while. Get out of the bath.'

'But... in my own house? What's going on?'

'I said get out!' Her voice was a whiplash, and he found himself obeying instantly.

'That's better. Now, put this on.' She handed him a collar from which hung a strap fitted with wrist restraints.

'Oh no, Esther mustn't know—'

'Put it on!' His hands moved, buckled it around his neck. 'Turn it around and put your hands behind you,' she commanded. Almost whimpering with fear – and excitement – he did so, and allowed her to buckle his wrists to the middle of his back. The front of the collar pulled on his throat, made him retch, and his erection flourished.

'Now, open your mouth.' She fed a ball gag between his lips and buckled it firmly. 'Now, what was it you were saying about Esther?' she mocked.

He groaned. He was finished. Esther would come in, find him trussed like a Christmas turkey at the whim of some strange woman and would request an instant divorce on the grounds of sexual perversion.

She patted the cheeks of his arse. 'Oh well,' she said, seemingly aware of his thoughts. 'You can't hide your light under a bushel all your life. The poor thing has to learn of your true nature at some time.'

She pulled a leather hood over his head, buckling him firmly into darkness. He choked briefly as her action forced the ball further into his mouth, then controlled it. What did she mean about Esther learning of his true nature?

'Good boy,' the woman purred. 'Now, I've another little toy for you. You'll like this. I bought it especially.' He jumped as she ran a sharp-nailed finger down the middle of his back, between his tensed buttocks, and pushed it briefly into his arse. His penis jumped. 'Turn around,' she ordered.

Reaching between his thighs, her fingers brushed enticingly against his aching balls. Despite his desperate predicament, he shuddered with delicious expectation, and sure enough, she pulled something back through, and as she pulled, something pressed against his anus and entered, sliding in slowly and inexorably. His nostrils flared within the hood as he inhaled deeply, stretched to accommodate whatever it was that penetrated his rectum.

She fiddled about below, and Kevin felt a sort of stretching and constricting as she tightened leather straps; separating, lifting and squeezing. Then she pulled a strap up to his chest and secured it to the collar. He wriggled experimentally. It felt awful – and it felt wonderful. A wide strap of leather bit into the cheeks of his arse, and he couldn't move a muscle without something pulling uncomfortably on his cock or balls.

'Nearly there,' she said.

He groaned. What next?

She ground his nipples between her fingers, and when he tried to back away she merely tugged the strap which went up his chest. He screamed behind the gag and stepped forward involuntarily as the full force of her persuasion nearly yanked off his undercarriage.

'You don't make a move unless I tell you to, slave,' she said easily. 'Is that clear?'

He nodded, and stood obediently still while she attached sprung clips to his nipples. From the strange tension he realised that those, too, must be attached to the rest of the kit.

'Now, you will walk forward,' she ordered.

With her hand offering gentle persuasion on the strap at the front, he was extremely careful. He cringed, knowing he was in his own house, going down his own stairs, and that Esther might come in at any moment and find him being humiliated by his mysterious woman – and not for the first time. He wanted to tell her to hurry, to get him out of the house and to wherever they were going.

They reached the kitchen without mishap, and he heard her open the door to the garage. Esther was the only one who ever used it – for the freezer, and paints and things – but he knew the geography of his own house. Had the black she-cat put her car in it, out of the way of prying neighbour's eyes? He fervently hoped so.

His bare feet padded quietly on the concrete floor, and she pulled him to a halt. 'Now, spread your legs and stand still,' she ordered curtly. He felt more straps being buckled tightly around his ankles, and the pressure of a stretcher between them. He wondered how she was going to get him in a car like that. 'Just one more refinement,' she said, and he felt his collar tighten even more.

Now what? He pulled, took an awkward step forward, felt everything tighten as whatever she had clipped to his collar held fast. What the hell was she about?

'You really are a rather nasty little man, aren't you?' the woman suddenly whispered with apparent loathing. He tensed, wondering if this was where she was going to beat him.

But the silence lengthened menacingly.

'You see,' she eventually said out of the darkness, 'I

thought it was time your poor wife got to know just what a worm you really are. I'm therefore going to leave you here for her to find.'

He made muffled, spluttering noises behind the mask.

'I expect you wondered who phoned you to say your wife was in hospital, didn't you?' she went on, patronising him.

He froze, waiting to hear more.

'I also phoned that dear innocent little secretary, Gloria, and told her that her boss had a dose of the clap. I don't think you'll be getting any joy with her, in future.'

Kevin clenched his fists behind his back. He'd love to get this woman's neck between them. He gave an angry pull at the tough leather, gasped, felt tears spring to his eyes, and waited, breath held, while the pain receded.

'Do you want to know what else I've done?' He didn't want to know, but she was going to tell him anyway.

'Well, I've written it all down. The hotels, the dates, the times. And I've left it all on your kitchen table.'

Kevin made a strangled, pleading noise.

'She's not stupid,' the taunting continued. 'She'll know what she reads is the truth. The time for retribution is at hand, Kevin. You may or may not like it, depending on how forgiving dear Esther turns out to be.' Her voice dripped sarcasm, and Kevin recalled using those very words not so long ago.

'Now, I am going to leave a few of my little toys here for your wife. The cane. The bullwhip. The electricity kit. Do you think she'll just come in and release you, Kevin? I don't. I'm sure she'll rise to the occasion in splendid style.' He sensed amusement. 'Probably you will too. Now, goodbye, sweetie.'

Sure enough she gave a parting tweak at his bonds, making him wince, before he heard her heels clack towards the door, into the kitchen, and away.

Oh, Jesus, he thought, and began to work at his bonds with utter desperation, only to realise it was hopeless.

He stood with his legs spread vulnerably in the chilly garage, unable to shuffle more than a step in each direction before something pulled unbearably.

But he couldn't just accept this humiliation; his naked vulnerability was almost as great a disaster as the letter awaiting Esther in the kitchen. So he twitched and turned, unwittingly causing the strategically placed straps, clips and bungs to do their dastardly work.

His betraying body tingled with the erotic sensation of leather pressed tight, and his cock swelled as the bung in his arse stretched and tantalised, and his nipples throbbed as the clamps tightened around the tortured buds.

Oh, the shame of it all. Not only was Esther going to return to find him like something out of a fetish magazine, but she was going to find him proudly and undeniably rampant. He felt like crying, because the discovery would utterly disgust her and drive her from him. It would be the end of their marriage, of that he was convinced. And that was something he'd never wanted.

He waited in silence, realising how unhappy he felt at the thought of losing his wife. Why had he been such an unfaithful prat?

The kitchen door slammed.

He tensed, holding his breath.

There was a long silence. She was reading the letter. He

whimpered. He heard soft footsteps padding towards the garage. There was another uncomfortably long silence. He turned his head to the direction of where he thought the door was. He heard a shocked gasp, and froze. He moaned, hung his head, wanting to hide. But he couldn't, so he stood there like a piece of meat for her to scrutinise, unable even to plead forgiveness.

'Kevin,' Esther eventually said quietly. 'Kevin, is that you under there?'

He made feeble noises of repentance.

'Oh my,' she gasped. 'Oh my, oh my!' He sensed her walk forward, but instead of releasing him she inspected the straps; looking, testing, seeing what moved what and what was attached to where. She brushed against the nipple clamps and touched the strap between his legs that held the plug in his arse.

'Oh my,' she said again. Only this time he heard the small hint of excitement in her voice.

Excitement? Esther?

He listened. She seemed to be walking away. No, she was coming back. He writhed in his bonds. He wanted to plead to be released, to be allowed to explain.

'Did you do all those things?' she asked softly. 'All those things I've just read?'

He shook his head frantically, making urgent noises.

'Liar,' she said firmly.

He felt the tentative bite of the cane on his thigh. He froze. Esther had hit him? Then it came again, harder. He could almost visualise her standing there, wondering how hard she could – or should – beat him. He could almost see her hardening features as she realised she could do exactly as she pleased to punish him – to extract revenge for the gory details she'd just had to read.

'Admit it,' she said. This time the cane bit deeper. He yelped, winced twice – once at the cane, the other because he had flinched a fraction too far.

He knew the next one was going to hurt. He heard the whistle. It landed across his buttocks and made him howl. He tried to turn away, but all he could do was to shuffle around – which he regretted as the next slash bit across his chest, catching one of his pulsing nipples. Through his pain he heard her give a grunt of satisfaction. She was enjoying it! His wife was beating the shit out of him, and was enjoying it! He yanked at the bonds. Just let him get free, and he'd show her who was boss...

But he couldn't free himself any more now than he could before, and the blows landed steadily and surely. Whichever way he shuffled he wished he hadn't as the cane found increasingly sensitive areas with alarming accuracy. She was not only enjoying it, he discovered, she was getting better at it.

His muffled cries were ignored, and the more she plied the cane and the more he danced the more the bondage came into play.

He wasn't sure at which particular stroke he lost his sense of righteous anger, his conception of the rights and wrongs of things; the point at which his body's sexual drive overwhelmed him, stopped him from thinking; the time when the slashes became a pleasure, and his constricted cock and balls were throbbing with a bursting need to be massaged.

His indignant cries turned to groans. Oh, touch me, he

was whimpering inside his head, and his hands were fingers were clenching and unclenching behind his back with the need to finish the job – with the pleasure of not being able to do so.

Suddenly, out of the darkness he sensed a change. She stopped beating him. He moaned again, but this time because he wanted her to carry on, to beat him into sexual submission. His erection was vast and in need of relief. What was she doing?

He gasped as she wrapped her arms around his neck, and he leaned back as she lowered herself onto his rampant cock, each leg lifted in turn and clenched around his hips. Once tightly wrapped against his trussed body she began to glide slowly up and down on his straining erection. It was all he could do to stand with his parted legs locked, his muscles straining as she rode him – as Esther, his wife, rode him like a seasoned breaker. He could do nothing but stand and accept, until the time came when his own tension rose like a geyser from within and could not be suppressed any longer. With gritted teeth and a heartfelt groan he shot his load, and with an equally loud cry Esther came too, wilting against his sweating chest, her face sinking to his sweating shoulder.

After a few minutes she climbed from him and they both breathed heavily in the silence. Fingers fumbled at his hood, lifted it a bit and removed the ball gag. He groaned with relief and worked some movement into his jaw.

'Esther... honey?' he eventually said tentatively.

There was a short silence, and then the unexpected swish of the cane. 'I've always hated being called honey,' she said venomously. 'I've told you that so many times and you just wouldn't listen. Well, now you have to listen, don't you?'

'Esther...' he simpered, 'will you let me down, please? I can explain.'

'Hah! This should be good,' she sneered. 'So, explain.'

He didn't like the cynicism he heard. 'Esther, it wasn't true, what that woman—!'

The vicious cut of the cane silenced him. 'Don't lie,' she said firmly. 'You are not in a very safe position for lying, are you?'

'Esther, you let me down this minute!' he ventured.

'I'll let you down when I'm good and ready.'

'Esther,' he said firmly. 'You don't know what you're saying. You're shocked, but I can—'

'Shut up.'

He couldn't believe his ears; couldn't believe the way his wife was talking to him and how she was behaving. 'Honey, this is all a silly mistake. Just let me—'

Again the savage cane cut him short.

'I warned you not to call me honey!'

The sting of the cane made him hiss. 'Esther... darling,' he croaked, 'I've been abused today—'

'The other women, the weekends away – they will, of course, stop immediately.'

'But—!' the cane cut down again and he lurched, the leather bonds creaking as he wailed in anguish.

'You'll learn eventually,' she said grimly. 'Now, the truth.'

Between the odd hint of less than gentle persuasion, he told all. His spirits sank lower and lower as he realised just how much that bitch had told his wife, how much she was just asking him to confirm.

'Now,' Esther said when he'd finished. 'Let's get one thing straight. If I let you go, you promise to be faithful to me?'

'I – I promise,' he said meekly.

'Because I've taken just about enough from you, and I won't have it any more.' She unbuckled the hood and pulled it from him completely.

Kevin blinked against the sudden light and frowned, confused. He was in his own garage, and yet... he was also in the lair of the bitch, and before him stood the bitch in person. In the same clothes as she had been wearing earlier, minus the lacy knickers. Very slowly, she reached up and removed her hood. 'Oh... my God,' he said in shocked wonder.

Esther smiled at him; a curious mixture of carnal knowledge and innocence. 'Yes, I'm the bitch,' she said. 'And from now on I will be a bitch whenever you need me to be. *And*,' she stressed, 'whenever you forget who you're married to.' She walked to the wall and released the ratchet that was holding him to the pulley system. 'You, in turn, will please me whenever I want you to.'

He stared at her, bemused. 'But I thought I did?'

'Well,' she said thoughtfully, 'after the dinner, in the woods – I have to admit you pleased me then.'

'You knew it was me? You didn't mind?'

Esther was delighted by the pitiful expression on her husband's face. He looked like a little lost boy. 'My dear,' she said, her confidence increasing all the time, 'I asked you to do it, and of course I enjoyed it – you were there, remember? I'm a red-blooded girl and I sometimes love to be tied up and rough sex, just like you do. Why you assume I won't like something when you do, I can't fathom.'

He tried to digest everything, his head in a spin. 'And in the van, you liked that?'

'Of course, silly,' she said, trying to disguise her astonishment. That had been him, too?

Now he was looking less worried, and more interested. 'And you want me to do things like that again?'

'Sometimes I'll just want you to make love to me, because I love you. But now and then I'll want you to tie me up and whip me as I tied you up and whipped you. I'll want you to abuse me. But most of all, from now on we are married in every sense of the word. Do you understand?'

Kevin lowered his eyes and nodded, suddenly feeling ashamed of his history of infidelity and cursing himself for foolishly ignoring his lovely wife and risking their marriage. As Esther knelt to release the ties around his ankles he gazed down at her beauty and felt breathless feelings of love well up inside. She really was quite a girl. He'd never fool around again.

Esther felt euphoric that her plan had achieved such a complete success. She just knew that she'd won her husband back, that from now on he'd be totally loyal and attentive, cherishing what he had. She glanced up and caught him looking down at her. Her wide eyes sparkled and her soft voice was seductive as she said, 'And as for the abduction in the van... that was a brainwave. I was so turned on...'

As soon as she'd spoken she knew something was

wrong. Kevin looked blank, and her stomach sank as he said, 'Abduction? What van?'

Exciting titles available from Chimera

1-901388-20-4	The Instruction of Olivia	*Allen*
1-901388-01-8	Olivia and the Dulcinites	*Allen*
1-901388-12-3	Sold into Service	*Tanner*
1-901388-13-1	All for Her Master	*O'Connor*
1-901388-14-X	Stranger in Venice	*Beaufort*
1-901388-16-6	Innocent Corinna	*Eden*
1-901388-17-4	Out of Control	*Miller*
1-901388-18-2	Hall of Infamy	*Virosa*
1-901388-23-9	Latin Submission	*Barton*
1-901388-19-0	Destroying Angel	*Hastings*
1-901388-21-2	Dr Casswell's Student	*Fisher*
1-901388-22-0	Annabelle	*Aire*
1-901388-24-7	Total Abandon	*Anderssen*
1-901388-26-3	Selina's Submission	*Lewis*
1-901388-27-1	A Strict Seduction	*Del Rey*
1-901388-28-X	Assignment for Alison	*Pope*
1-901388-29-8	Betty Serves the Master	*Tanner*
1-901388-30-1	Perfect Slave	*Bell*
1-901388-31-X	A Kept Woman	*Grayson*
1-901388-32-8	Milady's Quest	*Beaufort*
1-901388-33-6	Slave Hunt	*Shannon*
1-901388-34-4*	Shadows of Torment	*McLachlan*
1-901388-35-2*	Star Slave	*Dere*
1-901388-37-9*	Punishment Exercise	*Benedict*
1-901388-38-7*	The CP Sex Files	*Asquith*
1-901388-39-5*	Susie Learns the Hard Way	*Quine*
1-901388-40-9*	Domination Inc.	*Leather*
1-901388-42-5*	Sophie & the Circle of Slavery	*Culber*
1-901388-11-5*	Space Captive	*Hughes*
1-901388-41-7*	Bride of the Revolution	*Amber*
1-901388-44-1*	Vesta – Painworld	*Pope*
1-901388-45-X*	The Slaves of New York	*Hughes*
1-901388-46-8*	Rough Justice	*Hastings*
1-901388-47-6*	Perfect Slave Abroad	*Bell*
1-901388-48-4*	Whip Hands	*Hazel*
1-901388-50-6*	Slave of Darkness	*Lewis*
1-901388-51-4*	Savage Bonds	*Beaufort*
1-901388-53-0*	Wages of Sin *(Mar)*	*Benedict*
1-901388-54-9*	Love Slave *(Mar)*	*Wakelin*
1-901388-55-7*	Slave to Cabal *(April)*	*McLachlan*
1-901388-56-5*	Susie Follows Orders *(April)*	*Quine*

All **Chimera** titles are/will be available from your local bookshop or newsagent, or direct from our mail order department. Please send your order with a cheque or postal order (made payable to *Chimera Publishing Ltd*) to: **Chimera Publishing Ltd., PO Box 152, Waterlooville, Hants, PO8 9FS**. If you would prefer to pay by credit card, email us at: **chimera@fdn.co.uk** or call our **24 hour telephone/fax credit card hotline: +44 (0)23 92 783037** (Visa, Mastercard, Switch, JCB and Solo only).

To order, send: Title, author, ISBN number and price for each book ordered, your full name and address, cheque or postal order for the total amount, and include the following for postage and packing:
UK and BFPO: £1.00 for the first book, and 50p for each additional book to a maximum of £3.50.
Overseas and Eire: £2.00 for the first book, £1.00 for the second and 50p for each additional book.

*Titles £5.99. All others £4.99

For a copy of our free catalogue please write to:

Chimera Publishing Ltd
Readers' Services
PO Box 152
Waterlooville
Hants
PO8 9FS

Or visit our Website at:
www.chimerabooks.co.uk